JUNGLE TALES

Andy Yiangou

www.kingdompublishers.co.uk

Jungle Tales

A catalogue record for this book is available from the British Library

ISBN 978 - 0 - 9935959 - 0 - 5

First Published 2016 by
KINGDOM PUBLISHERS
London, England

Dedication

I want to thank first and foremost my Lord Jesus for making this book possible and for all his inspirations.

Secondly I dedicate this book to my children Joshua, Daniel and Benjamin. May they have many moments of joy when reading these stories.

CONTENTS

GREETINGS

Greetings from the Karoomba jungle, home to a bunch of mismatched animals you would never see in one place at the same time. Of course, I'm not including myself; I would say I am the most sophisticated of them all. Hence that's why I am narrating these tales... well, to be honest, no-one else wanted to do it. Well, Barbra the Baboon hinted, but never actually stepped forward; just as well, as I didn't think she would have been committed to the task. Anyway, please forgive my rudeness; I totally forgot to introduce myself: my name is Oliver the Owl. Wisest of the all the animals, so they say; I cannot argue with that, although some will beg to differ. So here I am, as narrator, and I have selected some of the funniest and craziest tales this jungle has ever witnessed and – believe me – you will agree. From lost treasure maps to wacky races to giant beanstalks, every tale is full of fun-filled adventures with a valuable lesson learned at the end. So what are we waiting for? Let's begin with my favourite member of the jungle: Lenny the Lion.

LENNY AND MICK

There was lots of excitement in the Karoomba jungle, as almost every animal was getting ready for Leo's birthday bash.

Lenny the Lion stood admiringly in front of his enormous mirror and roared proudly at the sight of his reflection.

"I'm so big, I'm so strong, I'm so handsome, he-high-he..." sang Lenny at the top of his voice, which was loud enough to disturb his neighbours' peaceful sunny afternoon, which consisted of doing absolutely nothing except filling their stomachs with cold jungle fruit juice.

George the Giraffe and Eric the Elephant lay on the lawn in their reclining deck chairs, drinking their fourth glass and taking in as much sun as they could.

"He sounds happy," whispered George taking a gulp of juice, which left froth on his top lip.

"I think he's excited about Leo's birthday party,"

replied Eric, emptying fruit juice from his trunk into his mouth.

"It's going to be a right old laugh tonight, Eric!" said George licking his lips with one swipe from his long tongue.

"It's sure going to be a great night!" shouted Lenny as he skipped and hopped past them, "and I'm starting early!"

"You think we should also get there early, you know, in case all the drink and food runs out?" suggested Eric.

"Nah, we've got plenty of time," said George filling Eric's glass to the top. "Knowing Leo, he's probably got enough food and drink to feed the world!"

"Mmm, you're right there, Georgie-boy," replied Eric, raising his glass at the thought of an ocean full of fruit juice, before dunking his trunk into it.

Leo the Lion, famous for owning the only juice parlour in the jungle, filled it every year with every jungle beast he knows in order to celebrate his birthday. Apart from Lenny, Leo's other close friends were Larry the Lion, Luther the Lion and Lester the Lion, and throughout the jungle they were known as the Pride, the most feared animals in the jungle... well, that is what they were led to believe. In fact, they couldn't frighten a fly off a pile of dung, let alone anyone else. Even so, everyone kept up the pretence, in order to gain access to Leo's juice parlour and his thirst-quenching beverages.

The sunlight, filtering through the treetops, brought tranquillity to the jungle as Lenny made his way towards Leo's juice parlour, humming merrily along with the enchanting sounds of the birds singing cheerfully to each other. You could feel a great sense of excitement around the rainforest as the mass gathering of every party animal the jungle could muster was about to descend upon the juice parlour.

Lenny halfway through his journey noticed something bright and shiny in the bushes. He tried to ignore it, but could not, as the curiosity was too much. This curiosity will kill me one day, he thought, as he went back to take a better look. He stood, looking down at the object for a moment, before bending down and grabbing it with his paw. It gave a little, but did not budge, so he used both paws and – with one mighty pull – it gave way. Then, in a second – just a second, which was all it took – Lenny found himself trapped in a cage.

"Me, a lion, in a trap, impossible, it can't be!" he roared, shaking the cage with fury.

He shook and pulled for almost an hour, before realising that the three-inch iron bars were not going to break. He fell into a crying heap, his strength totally drained from all his effort and the thought of the humiliation of being trapped plagued his mind.

"What will everyone think of me? I'll be the joke of the jungle," sobbed Lenny. "No lion ever gets trapped..." he added covering his face with his paws as he wept at the thought of his embarrassment.

"Can I help you?" squeaked a voice from inside the cage.

"Who's that?" said a startled Lenny as he stood up and looked around in bemusement.

"Oi, down here," replied the squeaky voice

Lenny looked down at the floor of the cage and there, looking straight back at him, was a little white mouse. Lenny licked his lips as his rumbling stomach reminded him that he was hungry and bent down to face the little snack. In fact, he got so close that both their noses touched, causing the mouse to swallow hard.

"Don't eat me, please don't eat me," pleaded the mouse, who spoke very quickly without a pause.

"Whyever not?" laughed Lenny.

"I can help you get out," replied the mouse bravely.

Lenny stood up and thought for a moment.

"How?" he asked. "How could someone so small get me out?"

"I'll chew through the bars; I've got strong teeth, you know," answered the mouse, now feeling a bit calmer.

"Alright then, give it a go," said Lenny feeling a little optimistic. "This I've got to see," he added, intrigued.

"Oh, great, I'm so pleased. My name's Mick, what's yours? If I help you, will you promise to love me and look after me forever and ever?" replied Mick in one breath.

"Will you, will you, will you, will you, will you, will you, will you, will you, will you, will you, will you, will you, will you, will you, will you, will you, will you, will you...?" continued Mick before Lenny could even open his mouth to speak.

"YES!" interrupted Lenny, covering both his ears with his paws. "Anything... just as long as you shut up!"

"Oh, I'm so happy, I'm so happy, it would be great: we could stay up late, eat snacks, sing and dance all night and watch the sun rise in the morning. Oh, how great it's going to be, we must celebrate, let's have a party, I could invite Matthew, Mark, Mario and Michael, oh, I'm so happy, I'm so happy, I'm so hap..."

"ENOUGH!" screamed Lenny.

"...py," said Mick finishing his sentence.

"I've got somewhere important to get to so, if you don't mind, I'll like to see those teeth of yours in action," said Lenny, remembering Leo's birthday party.

Mick made short work of the bars and soon Lenny was free.

"I'm freeeeeeeeeeeeeeeeeeeeeeeeeeeeeee," roared Lenny as he danced around, delighted that he was not seen by anybody.

"Let's party!" squeaked Mick who also was dancing around with joy at the prospect of late night singing and dancing and snacks.

"Let's eat!" replied Lenny, swinging a paw at Mick, who was fortunate to dive into a bush before he became lion food.

"You promised you promised you'll love me look after me forever and ever... you promised!" yelled Mick from under the bush.

"Ha ha, lions don't promise foolish mice," laughed Lenny, giving up the chase as he disappeared into the jungle towards Leo's juice parlour.

The parlour was full of joyful party animals from every corner of the jungle; even Oliver the Owl turned up this year, who often thought himself too sophisticated to attend. Most of the guests were regular customers, including Harry the Hyena, who couldn't stop laughing at Henry the Hippo, who broke the chair he was sitting on due to his weight. Everyone else, on the other hand, was having a great time in their own kind of way – like Chris the Cheetah who was trying to impress Claire the Cheetah and Charlotte the Cheetah by balancing a chair on his head; they instead focused their attention on Geoffrey the Gorilla, who was balancing a table and two chairs on his head, whilst beating his chest at the same time. As for Larry, Lester and Luther, they took it upon themselves to be the night's entertainment, singing merrily out of tune in the corner of the room to the rest of the guests.

The party was in full swing when Lenny finally walked in, and it was Leo who noticed him first and beckoned him over, holding a freshly-poured jug of fresh fruit juice.

"Where've you been?" asked Leo, passing over a plate of burgers and chips along with his juice.

"I got held up... but I'm here now," he replied, emptying the contents of the plate down his throat within seconds, before washing it all down with fruit juice. "Another juice, please..." he added, handing back his jug.

Lenny carried his drink over to the Pride who were still busy singing in deafening high- pitched voices, but stopped in his tracks a few feet from his mates.

"Hooray!" they cheered when they saw Lenny.

Lenny, instead, stood stunned with horror, mouth wide open (just like Charles the Crocodile, when he couldn't believe that Harold the Hare, who was odds-on favourite to finish ahead of Trevor the Tortoise in last year's Great World Animal Race, was beaten by Trevor who finished miles ahead. No-one expected the Tortoise to beat the Hare.)...

Standing on Larry the Lion's head and singing in an even greater high-pitched voice was Mick the Mouse. Lenny couldn't believe his eyes and with one swipe he tried to catch Mick, but instead missed and slapped Larry across the face. The Pride stopped singing, then the music stopped and then everyone turned and faced the Pride.

"What was that for?" said a bewildered Larry, stroking his face to ease the pain.

"I'm sorry, Larry, I didn't mean to hit you," replied Lenny apologetically. "I was after that mouse."

"What's Mick done to you?" said Larry.

"Yeah... what's he done?" said Luther and Lester together.

Lenny struggled to answer and out popped Mick from inside Larry's mane.

"He broke his promise," squeaked Mick.

"Promise? What promise?" asked Larry confused.

"He promised to love me and look after me forever and ever and ever," answered Mick.

"Aaaaaaaah!" replied the rest of the animals mockingly and adding to Lenny's embarrassment.

"Is that true?" Larry asked Lenny.

"I did no such thing," lied Lenny.

"You did, you did!" protested Mick. "Just before I rescued you when you got yourself trapped in that cage!"

"Rescued me from a cage? That's nonsense!" replied Lenny, trying to protect his ego.

"I did rescue him, he's lying; when I found him, he was trapped and crying his eyes out," said Mick sincerely, sealing Lenny's shame.

Lenny's red face spoke volumes – it was Harry the Hyena who was first to laugh, and before long, the whole parlour was full with cries of laughter.

"Why, you little rodent..." yelled an angry Lenny as he

grabbed Mick and dangled him by his tail over his mouth.

"HEEELP!" squeaked Mick as he was engulfed by a huge whiff of burgers, chips and a hint of fruit juice. "Are you crazy?" yelled Larry, snatching a dazed Mick from almost certain death.

Lenny noticed the whole place had become quiet and that he felt all eyes were on him. His humiliation was now complete and he made a rapid retreat to the exit. He stood outside for a moment; it was cold, dark and lonely but inside he could hear laughter, the loudest being from Harry the Hyena. He slowly turned back and faced the jungle, took a deep sigh, and began making the long journey home.

A year flew by and, once again, it was Leo's birthday party. The events from last year had slowly been forgotten after months of Lenny receiving endless teasing. Eric the Elephant finally landed a job in a bakery, only to get sacked the same day after eating almost half the stock. One cake turned to two, two turned to four and before long he had devoured twenty cream cakes, eleven jam doughnuts, fifteen currant buns and forty-five chocolate éclairs. George the Giraffe also found a job, but quit after a week so that he could join Eric on the lawn.

Once again, Lenny headed off to Leo's juice parlour, passing Eric and George on the way. A faint breeze accompanied him while he walked through the jungle, when something bright and shiny caught his eye. Curiosity once again got the better of him as he yanked and pulled until (yes, wait for it... yep, you guessed it!) he was trapped again.

"Nooooo, not again!" roared Lenny.

"Can I help you?" came a voice from the floor of the cage.

"Who are you?" asked Lenny, looking down at a little brown mouse.

"My name's Matthew; if I rescue you, will you promise to love me and look after me forever and ever?" squeaked Matthew.

The End

. . . .

It brings a smile to me every time I tell the tale. So, tell me: did Lenny learn from his mistake of investigating shiny objects? I don't think so, but Lenny had learnt a valuable lesson about humility the hard way. His pride had led him to believe that he was invincible and that he was greater than anything smaller and weaker than himself. Instead, he had to be humbled by a tiny mouse, which goes to show that if Lenny had showed humility to Mick, he would not have been humiliated in front of his friends when they found out that he had to get help from a tiny mouse.

What we learn from this story is that, no matter how thick the cage bars are, nothing is impossible with God and that we should always turn to him to help us when we are in need. We can also learn that we should not be too proud to accept help, especially if it comes from someone you think cannot. The Bible teaches us to lean on God's power and his guidance and not by our own strength. God will help us in many ways, including sending someone to help you, even though they may appear that they cannot.

James 4:10 and Luke 1:37

LAWRENCE

My second tale I remember quite well, as if it were yesterday; it was because of what happened that day that I promised myself: never again will I get involved in anything that these animals of this jungle do. I'm sure your curiosity levels have risen, so let me begin, right at the very beginning.

It was going to be yet another hot day in the Karoomba jungle as the sun shone brightly against a blue cloudless sky that morning. Surprisingly, Lenny the Lion was up, as he let out a yawn, which turned into a loud roar.

"Blimey, he's up early," said George the Giraffe to Eric the Elephant, as they both lay on their reclining chairs, drinking Eric's homemade tropical ice-chilled juice.

"I bet he's sleepwalking," said Eric.

"I don't think so," replied George, looking up at Lenny, who was leaning out of his bedroom window and breathing in the fresh air. "I think he must have hit his head and the knock's confused him!"

"What's got you up early?" asked Eric, intrigued at Lenny's sudden appearance in the morning. "Had enough sleep?"

"For your information, us lions need plenty of sleep to maintain our majestic beauty," replied Lenny, stroking back his mane.

"Majestic what?" laughed George

"Hey, Georgie-boy, I believe he thinks he's royalty!" joked Eric.

"Yeah, king of the jungle!" replied George mockingly.

"Laugh all you want, guys, but jealousy won't get you anywhere," said Lenny in his defence. "In fact, why would anyone find two buffoons like you two attractive, especially one with a long nose and another with a long neck?"

"You're in a good mood this morning, aren't you?" said George sarcastically.

"Jokes aside, Lenny, why are you up so early?" asked Eric, curious at Lenny's morning presence.

"Wouldn't you like to know?" replied Lenny, purposely delaying his answer.

"Oh, leave him, Eric; you know he's as stubborn as that pimple that keeps coming back on your bottom."

"I thought we weren't going to mention that again, ever!" replied Eric, embarrassed.

"If you'd really like to know, I'm expecting my long-distant cousin, Lawrence," interrupted Lenny. "He's due to arrive shortly."

"Long-distant cousin, you say?" queried Eric.

"Yes, he's my aunt's daughter's daughter's son's daughter's daughter's son, or something like that..." explained Lenny.

"Right, I see," replied a confused Eric.

"Apparently he likes to travel all over the world, and has been to almost eighty countries," explained Lenny, "and he's passing through here before he heads home," he added.

"He sounds like a bit of a nomad," said Eric.

"Have you ever met him?" asked George.

"Only once before, and he seemed a bit of an eccentric," said Lenny.

"Great, that's all we need, a stark raving lunatic prancing around our jungle, boring us all to death with his travelling adventures, which only he finds exciting," moaned Eric

"Since you guys have taken such an interest, can I ask a favour?" asked Lenny politely, coming up with an idea.

"Well, it all depends on what it is..." replied George.

Would you mind keeping an eye out for him while I' prepare breakfast?" asked Lenny, who knew they would agree, as both were as nosy as each other.

"We might as well, Georgie-boy, we're not exactly pushed for time" said Eric pushing deeper into his recliner.

"You might have a point there, Eric," replied George, doing the same.

"Yeah, why not, Lenny? We haven't got anything else to do, plus it would be interesting to meet your cousin," said Eric.

"Cheers, guys, I owe you one," replied Lenny, grinning joyously.

"I'd better go for more tropical juice," said Eric, picking up the two empty glasses,

"Make it a large one, Eric, you know Lions; they're not the most punctual of animals," chuckled George.

"I'd better see if I could find a straitjacket for old loopy Lawrence..." giggled Eric.

"Yeah, you better!" replied George, going along with the joke.

Lenny had no intention of making any sort of breakfast – well, not at that moment – instead he went straight back to bed, and before long, he was fast asleep, dreaming of eating a giant beef burger filled with tons of his favourite relish. While Lenny slept away, Eric and George waited for Lawrence, and soon they were joined by Wilbert the Wildebeest and Zed the Zebra.

"Morning George, morning Eric," greeted Wilbert, "another scorcher, hey?"

"It certainly is," replied George, before taking a huge gulp of tropical juice.

"Rumour has it that we're experiencing dramatic global warming," said Eric. "Something to do with cutting down trees, I think."

"How on earth do trees cause global warming?" asked a bewildered Zed.

"Beats me," said Eric, shrugging his shoulders.

"I bet it's those polar bears up north burning the trees to keep themselves warm," replied George, "still, I don't blame them, it must be freezing up there."

"Something's missing up there" said Wilbert, pointing to his head. "I don't know why they don't come down south to live if it's that cold."

"Too hot, apparently," replied Eric.

"Give me the sun and the heat anytime!" said Wilbert.

"I agree," replied George.

"Where are you two off this morning?" asked Eric.

"Nowhere, really, Zed and I thought of going down to the waterhole for a nice soak," answered Wilbert. "What about you two?"

"Nothing much, just sitting here drinking Eric's wonderful homemade tropical fruit juice and taking in the sun," answered George.

"And we're waiting for Lawrence," added Eric.

"Lawrence, who's Lawrence?" enquired Wilbert.

"Lawrence is Lenny's famous distant cousin, who has apparently travelled all over the world, to eighty countries, I think," explained Eric.

"He's a bit loopy as well," added George.

"I'm not surprised with all that travelling," said Zed, "he must be quite a character."

"I quite agree," said Wilbert, "I'd love to meet him."

"Sure, take a seat," replied Eric, ushering them to sit down.

"Marvellous," said Wilbert, excitedly. "I'll have some of that homemade juice too!"

"Mmmm, me too!" said Zed, licking his lips at the prospect.

"Same again, George?" asked Eric.

"Don't mind if I do!" answered George, passing over his glass.

Eric went off to make more of his tropical juice. An hour later, he returned with four glasses and, to his surprise, Henry the Hippo, Aaron the Aardvark, Philip the Panda, Betty the Bobcat and Charlie the Chimpanzee had all joined in the wait. "I think I'd better make more," moaned Eric.

"You'd better fill that old barrel, Eric; it looks like we could be expecting more visitors," replied George.

In fact, George was right; it was not long before James and Janet the Jaguars, who were out for a morning stroll, came over to find out what all the commotion was about.

"What's with the gathering?" asked James.

"For Lawrence," answered Charlie the Chimpanzee.

"Who's Lawrence?" asked Janet.

"You know... Lawrence?" insisted Charlie.

"No, we don't," replied James, honestly.

"Pity you" replied Charlie cheekily.

"Why? What's so special about Lawrence that brings such a crowd to welcome him?" asked James.

"Yeah, I would love to know," said Janet curiously.

"Well apparently he's famous for going crazy after trying to travel the world in eighty days," said Charlie.

"Did he do it?" asked James, intrigued.

"From what I heard, yes," answered Charlie.

"In that case, I think I'll wait as well," said James. "What do you say, Janet dear?"

"Why not?" agreed Janet, excitedly.

So Janet and James joined the rest of the crowd, who were all busy enjoying Eric's homemade tropical fruit juice, of which he had made a huge barrel. Shortly after Janet and James's arrival, Paul the Porcupine, Wesley the Wolf, Charles the Crocodile, Raymond the Raccoon,

Fernando the Fox and Harry the Hyena had arrived, and all joined in to wait for Lawrence.

By midday the heat had intensified, as the jungle animals had drunk through two full barrels of tropical fruit juice. Eric, being near to exhaustion, got help from Philip the Panda to keep up the supplies; thankfully George came up with the idea to charge a small fee for each cup, the idea stopped Eric complaining and was then happy to make more fruit juice, since he was also making a small fortune.

Soon Olivia the Ostrich and Erica the Emu turned up, attracted by the crowd.

"What's going on here, then?" Olivia asked Harry the Hyena.

"We're all waiting for the one and only famous Lawrence!" answered Harry

"Never heard of him," replied Olivia, bluntly.

"What's he famous for?" Erica asked.

"He's famous for capturing eighty crazy bandits from all over the world," explained Harry.

"Wow, that's amazing!" replied Erica. "What do you say, Olivia dear? Shall we wait here for Lawrence?"

"You try and stop me, Erica dear!" insisted Olivia.

"Oh, wonderful! I've never met anyone famous! I'm

ever so excited!" replied Erica, blissfully.

"Me neither... and so brave and all!" replied Olivia joyously. "Oh... Erica, dear, are my feathers all nice and straight?" she asked, looking behind at her tail feathers.

"Elegant as always," giggled Erica, "what about mine?"

"Not a feather out of place!" replied Olivia truthfully.

"Oh, jolly good!" said Erica cheerfully. "Now who's serving the tea?"

"Tea?" replied Harry, bemused. "We've only tropical fruit juice here."

"Tropical what?" said Erica and Olivia together, in horror.

"Tropical fruit juice," said Harry again. "It's quite good."

"I heard what you said, why is there not any tea? Don't you know that we're not just your average birds," remonstrated Olivia, "and I...?" "I understand," interrupted Harry. "I'll see what I can do..."

"Good! Some scones would be nice too!" said Olivia cheekily.

Olivia and Erica's request was granted by a disgruntled Eric, who brought tea for everyone and warm crumpets covered with sweet honey, which everybody, including Olivia and Erica, enjoyed a great deal. Soon they all were in high spirits as they entertained themselves with singing and a bit of dancing. Lenny, on the other hand, still remained sound asleep, unaware of the multitude of animals partying beneath his bedroom window.

As the day dragged on, and the sun continued to scorch the inhabitants below, more animals (drawn by the sound of the out-of-tune singing) joined in the fun, and soon word was out around the jungle of a party. In addition to who was already there, Brian the Bear, Koulla the Koala, Pete the Panther, Lars the Leopard, Ronald the Rhino, Barbra the Baboon, Marcia the Mongoose, and Otis the Orang-utan all arrived, bringing food and drink of their own. Even Oliver the Owl found the time away from his books to come and wait for Lawrence, joining in the fun.

"Who's having a party and didn't invite us?" asked Billy the Bison angrily when he turned up, together with Bruno the Buffalo.

"Yeah, I'm in the mood for crushing some heads!" said Bruno furiously.

"Please, it wasn't my idea..." pleaded Otis.

"Then whose was it?" asked Billy again.

"Nobody's," answered Otis, shrugging his shoulders. "We're all here waiting for Lawrence."

"Who's Lawrence?" asked Billy.

"Lawrence is one not to be messed with," replied Otis.

"No one's as tough as me and Billy!" yelled Bruno angrily.

"I won't argue with that," agreed Otis, "but apparently

he's a very dangerous crazy bandit who has killed over eighty animals from all over the world," he added bravely.

"Is he, now?" replied Bruno, unperturbed by what Otis had said about Lawrence.

"And from what I've heard, he's coming for Lenny, that's why we're all here to protect him," explained Otis.

"Well that's it then, looks like you're gonna need us," boasted Bruno. "What do you say, Billy, are you ready for some action?"

"You know me, Bruno, I'm always ready!" replied Billy, flexing his muscles.

Billy and Bruno were the last animals to join the crowd and, as the hours went by and the heat soared well into the nineties, the party atmosphere began to turn sour as tempers began to flare. One argument led to two and, before long, arguments had spread throughout the crowd. So it was only a matter of time before fights broke out, and they did, and you can guess who was relishing every moment of it. Billy and Bruno were straight in the thick of it, punching the life out of everyone who got in their way; Ronald the Rhino was sitting on Brian the Bear, bending back his arms, while Barbra the Baboon sat on his back, pulling back his ears. Charlie the Chimpanzee, Raymond the Raccoon and Koulla the Koala were on the receiving end of Paul the Porcupine's quills, and Olivia the Ostrich and Erica the Emu were kicking anyone who got too close. With the punching, kicking, biting and scratching and with Lenny in dreamland above tucked cosily in his bed, no one saw Lawrence arrive.

"Excuse me," said Lawrence, tapping the shoulder of Otis the Orang-utan who had kept well away from the fighting. "What's going on?""Everyone's gone crazy all of a sudden!" replied Otis.

"Why have they all gathered here in the first place?" asked Lawrence, intrigued.

"We're all waiting for the bandit," answered Otis.

"The bandit?" replied Lawrence curiously.

"Apparently, from what I hear, a very dangerous Bandit is coming for Lenny," explained Otis; "that's why we've all come here to protect him."

"I must go to Lenny straight away," replied Lawrence with a tone of urgency in his voice. "Can you tell me where I could find his house?"

"Sure, he lives over there," replied Otis.

"Thank you kindly," said Lawrence politely, quickly heading towards Lenny's house.

"Wait a second, who are you?" asked Otis nervously.

"I'm Lawrence," replied Lawrence quietly.

"D-d-did y-y-you s-say L-L-Lawrence?" stuttered Otis fearfully.

"Yes, that's correct," replied Lawrence politely.

"Everybody, everybody, it's Lawrence! Lawrence is

here!" screamed Otis as loud as he could.

The fighting stopped immediately and there was silence amongst the animals as everyone froze on the spot, unsure what to do, as they all had mixed feelings about Lawrence. Some were excited; others were curious; some were afraid; others wanted him dead.

"Kill him!" shouted Billy, breaking the silence.

"Yeah, kill him!" yelled Bruno.

"No, he's famous!" screamed Betty the Bobcat.

"Yes, kill the crazy fool!" shouted Wesley the Wolf.

"No, he's a hero! Spare him!" pleaded Olivia.

"Kill the crazy bandit!" yelled Billy, louder.

Lawrence did not wait around to ask any questions, nor did he try to reason with the horde of jungle animals racing towards him. Instead he ran as fast as his legs could carry him and disappeared into the jungle, never to be seen again.

Two days later, Lenny received a letter from Lawrence, explaining that he came to visit and was chased by some crazy animals who had mistaken him for a bandit. He carried on explaining that he had never had such a reception on his travels before, and had sworn never to visit Lenny again. Lenny did ask Eric and George about what happened... but, as they said, they just couldn't understand.

The End

Lenny did write to Lawrence to apologise and to reassure him that it was all a misunderstanding but it was all in vain. As for the animals, things went back to normal. Erica and Olivia still hoped to meet someone famous, and Leo the Lion heard about Eric's tropical fruit juice, and is now selling it in his fruit juice parlour. Lawrence eventually retired from travelling and is now living on his own on an island, telling no-one its whereabouts, and, as for Lenny, he promised himself that he would not sleep for so long... a promise that only lasted fifteen minutes. And, for the record, in case you were wondering, I never took part in any of the fighting or spreading any rumours about Lawrence... in fact, I was only there for Eric's very nice jungle juice.Anyway, the Bible teaches us that it is a sin to gossip and not to do it. In the story there was so much gossiping about Lawrence that the story about him changed. What happens with gossiping is that it can lead to rumours, which could be very damaging to the person who is talked about. Friendships, trust, and relationships can be lost, and fights and arguments can start, just by a few spoken words. The best thing to do is not to get involved with gossiping or any sort of conversation that speaks badly of someone, but also, remaining quiet means you agree what has been said, so it is always best to stand up for what is right and remember – if the person is not there to defend themselves – do not entertain any gossip. Sometimes it could be best not to hang around with gossipers.

Proverbs 16:28, 20:19, 26:20-22 and 2 Corinthians 12:20.

MAGIC BEANS

I learned a lot from this tale about the characters of many of the animals. Some behaved how I expected them to, but some really surprised me.

After days of heavy rain, the Karoomba jungle's inhabitants were much relieved to see the sun that morning. Eric the Elephant and George the Giraffe, long deprived of what they loved doing, did not waste any time, as they took out their recliners to catch the morning sun.

"This is more like it, Georgie-boy," said Eric, breathing in the fresh morning air through his trunk. "Yeah, I thought the rain would never stop," replied George, leaning back into his recliner.

"Don't you two ever get bored sitting out here all day?" asked Stuart the Stork, as he delivered the mail.

"Bored? How can we get bored with such a wonderful view, great weather and that halfwit lion to keep us entertained?" replied Eric.

"You have a point," said Stuart, "but don't you ever want to get a job?"

"We've tried that and found that jobs don't seem to like us," replied George.

"More like we don't like jobs!" Eric joked.

"You may have a point there, Eric!" laughed George.

"What you two need is a spell in the army; that should sort you both out," said Stuart.

"The army? I don't think so, not with my vertigo!" replied Eric.

"I'm short-sighted, so that counts me out," said George.

"As you see, Stuart, as much as we'd like to join the army, we wouldn't be eligible for selection anyway," said Eric.

"That's a shame, you both would have really benefited from the army," said Stuart sympathetically.

"Yeah, never mind, we'll get over it," said Eric, pretending to be bothered.

"Any mail for us?" asked George.

"Not today, I'm afraid," replied Stuart, regretfully. "This one's for Lenny."

"That's alright, Stuart, you know what they say: 'no news is good news'," laughed George.

"Well, if you put it that way, who can complain?"

replied Stuart, posting Lenny's letter.

Lenny woke around noon, but stayed in bed for another hour before he finally got up to make his breakfast/lunch of meatballs covered with tomato and basil sauce, one of his favourites. After finishing his meal, he turned his attention to the letter that Stuart had delivered. He knew straight away who had sent it as he looked at the envelope and, with a huge grin, he opened the letter. Just as he thought, it was from his very rich auntie, Lorraine the Lioness, who was inviting him to her very luxurious birthday party. The letter read:

TO LENNY

YOU HAVE BEEN INVITED TO CELEBRATE THE BIRTHDAY OF

HONOURED LIONESS LORRAINE

ON SATURDAY 4TH SEPTEMBER

AT THE BALMORAL MANSION

Fruit champagne reception at 7pm, followed by dinner and exquisite entertainment.

Very Smart dress recommended.

Lenny jumped with excitement at the prospect of yet another one of his auntie's parties. The thought of all the different luxurious foods thrilled him even more as he danced and sang around his living room. Lenny had every right to be filled with joy, as his auntie always hired the finest chefs to cook for her birthday parties. It was also an opportunity to visit the Saroomba Jungle, home of the exclusively rich and famous.

Saturday could not have come any sooner for Lenny, and when it finally arrived, he was up at the crack of dawn, in high spirits, preparing for his long journey to the Saroomba jungle. After packing his one and only dinner suit, his auntie's present and a few ham sandwiches for the long journey, he left, humming merrily to himself, passing George and Eric on his way.

"Crikey, Eric, he must be sleepwalking!" said George, surprised to see Lenny up so early.

"You lost track of time, or have all your clocks stopped working?" Eric joked.

"Funny, very funny," replied Lenny.

"Well, where are you off to, then, at this time of a morning?" asked Eric.

"Actually, I'm off to the Saroomba jungle" bragged Lenny.

"Saroomba jungle?" replied George, surprised. "You've finally won the Lottery then, Lenny?" asked George mockingly.

"I'm off to dine with the rich and famous, if you really must know," answered Lenny joyfully.

"You're pulling our leg!" said George, refusing to believe Lenny.

"You remember my rich aunt, Lorraine, who came and visited me last year?" said Lenny.

"How could we forget? It was like she was walking on stilts, the way she looked down at me and Eric," replied George.

"Oh, don't exaggerate," said Lenny, defending his aunt.

"Don't exaggerate? The way she looked at me and Eric, you would have thought we were some decaying lumps of flesh," said George honestly.

"Now you're being stupid," replied Lenny.

"Stupid? You wait; when you see her, you'll see," insisted George.

"Anyway, my auntie's having a birthday party," answered Lenny

"Lucky you," said Eric, sarcastically. "Don't forget her present..."

"Don't worry, I have it here," Lenny replied "now, if you don't mind, I have to be going... goodbye!" he added before walking off.

"Give our love to your aunt, now!" George shouted back.

"Yeah, give her our best wishes!" added Eric.Lenny continued on pretending not to hear them and soon Eric and George's witty remarks slowly fell silent and all Lenny could hear was the sound of the jungle birds singing cheerfully to themselves. Despite the journey being long, Lenny always found it quite a pleasant and enjoyable trek though beautiful, plush, dense jungle, around beautiful, serene lakes and up grass-covered hills, where he sat to eat his ham sandwiches whilst capturing the breathtaking view of the surrounding countryside.

It was just after seven when he arrived at his aunt's mansion in the middle of the Saroomba jungle. He quickly dressed into his suit before making his way through the huge iron gates towards the mansion. He walked up the path towards the marquee, where there were already many guests enjoying the fruit champagne and hors d'oeuvres. There he saw many of his aunt's rich friends and amongst them were some famous animals that Lenny recognised instantly. There was Boris the Bear, the greatest boxer who ever lived, Joe the Jackal, Grassland Jackals' former centre-forward who had the record for scoring over two hundred goals for one football team, and the great actors Kirk the Kangaroo and Selina the Sheep.

It suddenly went quiet when he entered the tent, which made him feel very uncomfortable as he felt every pair of eyes fall upon his old dinner suit. It was then that he remembered what George had said. Thankfully, his auntie noticed him, and quickly went to his rescue before Lenny made for the exit to escape his embarrassment.

"Lenny, dear, so glad you could make it," said Lorraine, delighted.

The guests resumed what they were doing a moment ago, idly chattering and drinking glass after glass of fruit champagne.

"Happy to be here," replied Lenny, glad to see his aunt.

"Everyone, this is my dearest nephew, Lenny," said Lorraine as she introduced Lenny to her guests, some of whom mumbled a greeting, whilst others just gave a fake smile.

"Come, dear, help yourself to fruit champagne; we'll be having dinner soon," said his aunt, ushering him over to the table that was full of tasty hors d'oeuvres. "It's a shame your mother couldn't make it again," she complained.

"You know Mother, she never was one to travel," replied Lenny. "This is for you," said Lenny, giving his aunt her present.

"Oh, thank you," answered Lorraine, taking the vase he bought her and handing it over to a servant, without looking at it.

He eventually cheered up when the food was served and, with the entertainment that later followed, his treatment by his aunt's guests was soon forgotten. He knew that the guests were just being nice for the sake of his aunt and that, behind his back, they were mocking his old dinner suit. Even his aunt pretended that she liked the vase that he bought her. Now he knew why his mother never attended his aunt's birthday parties. Still, Lenny was prepared to make the most of it, getting autographs from the famous and eating and drinking to his heart's content, until his stomach could fit no more.

Lenny woke up the next day feeling the effects of last night's overindulgence in rich food. It was well into the afternoon when he eventually emerged from the bedroom. Sensing that he was outstaying his welcome, he packed his old suit and made his goodbyes. His aunt, who cheerfully handed him some salmon sandwiches for his journey back, was quick to usher him to the gate; before long, his aunt's mansion was out of view.

It had become a miserable, gloomy day as the sun had disappeared behind the clouds threatening rain. Lenny had not noticed; instead, he was deep in thought about the way he had been treated, just for not being from the same class as his aunt's guests. This had made him more determined to get rich and make something of himself, so that he could fit in with the upper class. He was so focused on his thoughts on ways to become rich that he was unaware he was going the wrong way and, when he did realise, it was too late: he was completely lost in an unfamiliar jungle. He tried in vain to find the path back but, the more he tried, the more lost he became. After hours of wandering around the thick jungle, exhaustion forced him to stop. He found a rock to sit on, took out the salmon sandwiches his aunt had made, and ate them while he figured out how to find his way back. It was then that he noticed something in the distance. He moved closer for a better look and discovered a small stone bridge with a stream beneath it. Lenny smiled, for he knew that once he crossed the stream he would eventually find his way home.

"Stop right there!" yelled a voice which startled Lenny, who was about to step onto the bridge. "This is my bridge!"

Lenny paused with fear for a moment before summoning the courage to speak.

"I only want to pass," replied Lenny.

"None can pass unless I say so," said the voice firmly.

"Well, can I pass?" asked Lenny, feeling bolder.

"No," replied the voice.

"Why not?" enquired Lenny.

"No!" repeated the voice.

"Why don't you show yourself?" replied Lenny, beginning to lose his patience.

"What for?" replied the mysterious owner of the bridge.

"Well, one: I'd like to see who I'm talking to... and two: if you're much smaller and weaker than me, I'm going to give you such a beating for wasting my time," said Lenny angrily.

"Ooh, who's a touchy so-and-so, then?" said the voice, antagonising Lenny.

"Right, that does it! I'm crossing this bridge whether you like it or not!" threatened Lenny.

"You'd better not," warned the voice.

"Or what?" dared Lenny.

"Take one step further onto my bridge and you'll see," the voice warned again.

Lenny, who was not one to take any threats, took one step onto the bridge; as he waited, nothing happened. He then took several more steps until he reached the middle.

"What are you going to do now then, hey?" taunted Lenny as he danced around the bridge.

"I'm going to teach you never to step onto my bridge again," replied the voice, which came from behind Lenny.

Lenny quickly turned around to face the voice and saw an old goat swinging a walking stick around his head and, before Lenny could say anything, the goat – with all the strength he could muster – hit poor Lenny on the head with it. It took Lenny a few seconds to get over the initial shock, and then he felt the pain.

"I'm going to rip you from limb to limb" roared Lenny, grabbing the old goat with both paws.

"Please don't hurt me, please spare the life of an old goat," pleaded the goat.

"Why should I not teach you a lesson?" yelled Lenny.

"I can give you something that might interest you," said the old goat frantically.

"What can an old goat like you give a strong Lion like me?" boasted Lenny.

"Something that will make you rich," replied the old goat.

Lenny immediately released the old goat at his unexpected, but highly appealing, reply.

"Tell me, old goat," ordered Lenny.

"I will, but you promise you won't hurt me," replied the goat, "and the name's Gus."

"It depends on what you have to offer..." replied Lenny.

"Well, a month ago, a distant traveller – a lion like yourself – gave me these beans in exchange for crossing my bridge," explained Gus the Goat, "and he said..."

"Stop there for a minute," interrupted Lenny. "Before you carry on, what's with this bridge?" he asked curiously.

"This bridge has been in my family for generations – ever since my great-great-great-great-grandfather removed the troll who kept guard at this bridge, and since then, we continued doing the same," explained Gus.

"Troll? There's no such things as trolls!" laughed Lenny.

"There is," said Gus."There's not," replied Lenny firmly.

"There is," said Gus, adamant.

"Not," replied Lenny stubbornly.

"Is."

"Not."

"Is."

"Not."

"Is."

"Okay, okay, we could be here all day," said Lenny having had enough of the pointless argument, "why don't we agree to disagree?"

Gus thought for a moment before he replied, "Okay... but there is."

"You may continue telling me about this traveller," said Lenny changing the subject.

"As I was saying," continued Gus, "a distant traveller wanted to cross my bridge and, as usual, I wouldn't let him. But he was persistent and said he had to get as far away from the Karoomba jungle as possible, and insisted that I should let him pass in exchange for these magic beans, that can make whoever has them in their possession very rich."

"How'd you know that he wasn't pulling your leg?" asked Lenny.

"I don't; he seemed genuine enough, so I took his word for it," replied Gus.

The large bump on Lenny's head reminded him that Gus the Goat deserved a right old beating, but the thought of wealth was too much of a temptation, so he agreed to take the beans and spare the old goat.

Lenny arrived home late that night, exhausted by his extra-long journey, and (with a very painful head) he fell flat onto his bed and dozed off straight away. The next afternoon, after a night of dreams of a luxurious lifestyle of wealth and prosperity, he woke up feeling very optimistic about the prospect of becoming rich, picked up the beans and left the house to brag about his good fortune to all his friends.

"Good afternoon, guys, and what a wonderful day it is!" said Lenny as he passed Eric and George in very high spirits.

"Err, if you say so," replied Eric, looking up at the grey, gloomy sky.

"Don't tell me the aristocrats treated you like royalty?" George joked.

"You can joke all you want, but soon, I'll be richer then all my auntie's friends put together," replied Lenny.

"Blimey, Lenny; they've really messed up your head," said Eric.

"So what money-making scheme are you planning to do to make your fortune?" asked a very intrigued George.

"With these," replied Lenny, showing George and Eric the beans.

They both looked at the beans, paused for a moment, and then burst into laughter.

"What are you planning to do? Create a bean factory?" George joked.

"Maybe they're really antique beans, worth millions,"

mocked Eric.

"Yes, you've got it, Eric, I can see the rarity!" laughed George.

"Funny, very funny, but let's see who has the last laugh when I'm rolling in the green," replied Lenny, confidently.

"The only green you'll be rolling in is our lawn!" replied Eric, before bursting into fits of laughter.

Lenny ignored them and left for Leo's fruit juice parlour, thinking his mates would understand about his good fortune, but how wrong he was. Instead, all the Pride members laughed, including Geoffrey the Gorilla, Fernando the Fox, Claudia the Camel and – the loudest and most annoying of them all – Harry the Hyena. Lenny left the bar dejected and discouraged, his hopes of wealth beyond imagination shattered.He spent the remainder of the day alone on his favourite rock that overlooked the beautiful lush Karoomba jungle below. After watching the sun set, he went home quietly to sleep after hours of quiet and peaceful solitude and pleasant thoughts of life as a millionaire. When he reached his home, he was shocked to find that painted across the whole side of his house – in very big red letters – were some words.

The jungle's richest animal lives here!"You wait till I get hold of you, Gus," roared Lenny, "you'll wish you were never born a goat!"

Lenny, filled with rage, stormed straight into his room, took one look at the beans, and threw them out of his bedroom window.

How could I be such a fool to believe that old goat that beans could ever make me rich? Lenny thought. Because of him, I've become a laughing stock in all the Jungle. How could I ever show my face again?He lay agonisingly awake for most of the night at the thought of all the mockery he'd faced during the day, and the sound of the heavy rain did not help either, but eventually his tired mind gave up and he finally dozed off.

Lenny was awoken the next morning by a commotion outside his house. He leapt from his bed and ran to his window, only for his view to be completely covered by the huge leaves of an enormous plant. When Lenny made his way outside, he found a large crowd of jungle animals all looking gobsmacked up at the plant, which had grown endlessly towards the sky and beyond.

"Where did this come from?" asked Lenny, completely astonished at what he was looking at.

"We all thought of asking you the same question," replied Oliver the Owl, who was perched on top of Henry the Hippo's head.

"Believe me, I'm just as baffled as you are," said Lenny.

"Well, wherever it came from, that's the biggest beanstalk I've ever seen," said Oliver.

"Did you say beanstalk?" asked Lenny.

"I sure did – this is definitely a beanstalk," answered Oliver.

"The magic beans..." Lenny muttered under his breath.

It all made sense to Lenny, after remembering that he had thrown out the beans the night before, and with the help of the recent downpour, it had grew to an enormous size, to Lenny's – and everyone's – amazement.

More and more jungle animals began to appear, and it soon started to get out of hand thanks to Charlie the Chimpanzee, who had enticed some to climb the beanstalk; before long, there were jungle animals all over Lenny's garden, trampling all over his flowerbeds. This made Lenny very mad and, without hesitation, he threw them all out of his garden. After a while they all lost interest, and the crowd slowly began to disperse. "Well, those beans were magic after all," said George sarcastically. "You're a rich lion now."

"Yeah, Lenny; look at all that green," replied Eric, pointing at the beanstalk.

Lenny ignored them and tried to mend his flowerbed the best he could, whilst also trying to figure out how he was going to get rid of the beanstalk.

It took Lenny the rest of the day to sort out his garden, despite having to put up with George and Eric's continual jokes. After eating his dinner, he went straight to bed, as he planned to get up early to cut down the huge plant.

The next morning Lenny woke hoping that the giant beanstalk was all a dream, but as he looked towards his window, he soon learnt it was no dream; the beanstalk was real enough. After a long, relaxing stretch, he got up, determined to cut down the huge monstrosity that grew in his garden.

"I'll soon fix you", said Lenny quietly to himself, walking over to the window.

To Lenny's relief no crowd had gathered, surprisingly not even George and Eric. As he looked out of his window he noticed something different about the beanstalk. He took a closer look and saw that it was full of pods.

"Mmm, beans for breakfast," he said, pulling one off the beanstalk.

With one claw he popped open the pod, and what he saw left him dumbfounded. Out of the five beans, one of them was gold in colour. He picked up the gold bean and, to his amazement, it was solid gold. In his excitement he grabbed another pod and, again, one of the beans was gold. Again he grabbed another and, again, a gold bean. Frantically he began picking all the pods he could reach from his window; all had gold beans within.

"I'm rich, I'm rich!" yelled Lenny dancing around his room, tightly clutching his newly-found treasure.

At that moment, he remembered the rest of the beanstalk, quickly stopped dancing, and ran to the window.

"Blimey, there must be millions of them," said Lenny looking up and down the beanstalk, which was completely full of pods.

Lenny could not have moved any more swiftly to his cupboard as he rummaged around to find several sacks. Once outside, he began to pick frantically at every bean pod he could find, before anyone saw him. But that was soon to change as George and Eric found their place on the lawn.

"Looks like you've found some use for that beanstalk after all," said George.

"Looks like you're eating beans for a year there," said Eric.

Lenny pretended not to hear and continued to pick pods, hoping they would lose interest and leave him to it.

"I said, 'you'll be eating beans for a year'..." repeated Eric, this time louder.

Again Lenny ignored Eric.

"He's too busy, Eric; maybe he could do with a hand," said George.

"Need a hand?" asked Eric loudly

"No I'm fine, I can handle it," replied Lenny, trying to deter them from the idea of helping him.

"You're joking, right?" replied Eric.

"No, I'm fine, really," insisted Lenny.

"But there's thousands of them," Eric pointed out.

"I said, I'm fine," yelled Lenny.

"Alright, we're only trying to help!" replied Eric, feeling slightly aggrieved by Lenny's reaction.

The simple reason behind Lenny's behaviour was that

he wanted all the gold beans for himself and he knew that, if George and Eric found out, the whole Karoomba jungle would shortly find out too, and the thought of that brought him great fear.

While Lenny continued to pick as if his life depended on it, down below on the ground, Lenny's antics were getting noticed as several jungle animals had appeared.

"What's up with Lenny?" asked Janet the Jaguar. "Got a craving for beans, has he?"

"Beats me," replied Eric, "but whatever you do, don't ask to help."

"Wouldn't dream of it," replied Janet. "You wouldn't find me up there; those branches don't look safe."

"He looks kind of tired," said James the Jaguar.

"Maybe I should help him," said Barbra the Baboon.

"I'd better not, he's already upset Eric," said George.

"That's strange, I would have thought Lenny would jump at the chance of some help," said Philip the Panda.

"That's exactly what I thought," replied Eric.

"I'm going to ask him." said Barbra "Hey, Lenny, I'm coming up to help!" she yelled.

"No, don't; I'm fine," yelled back Lenny, who by now was quite high up.

"Why not?" replied Barbra."I said I was fine, so don't even think about climbing my beanstalk!" replied Lenny sternly.

"Well I never! I've never been spoken too so rudely in all my life," replied Barbra, deeply offended.

"Get over it," said Lenny, as he climbed down carrying a sackful of pods, locking them for safekeeping in his house.

"Hey, that's not nice, you've really upset her, you know," said Philip when Lenny re-emerged from his house.

"Give her a banana; that will cheer her up," replied Lenny as he made his way back up the beanstalk.

"Oh!" replied Barbra before bursting into tears.

"I don't understand; this isn't like Lenny," said George.

"You're right, Georgie-boy; this is all so strange," replied Eric.

By the time Lenny had filled up another sack, word had filtered through the jungle and, before long, a small crowd had gathered, including his Pride friends, Leo, Larry, Luther and Lester, and – as expected – they all heard what had happened to Barbra and, naturally, were supportive and began to remonstrate with Lenny. Lenny just ignored them and continued picking until he could find no more, even though the beanstalk continued further.

"I hope you're going to share some of those beans with us," said Leo.

"Yeah, I love beans," added Larry.

"No; they're all for me!" replied Lenny, making his way down.

"You're joking?" said a surprised Leo.

"He's not joking," replied George.

"You've got loads, from what I hear," said Luther, "several sacks full."

"If you can take a look at where the beanstalk is growing, you will notice that it is in my garden, which means that it belongs to me and, since it belongs to me, that means that everything that is on the beanstalk, which I should remind you all once again, belongs to me: IS MINE!" explained Lenny firmly and loudly.

"This isn't like you, Lenny, we're your mates," replied Leo sorrowfully.

"Mates? Only when you want something from me," replied Lenny.

"That isn't true, Lenny, and you know it," said Luther, to the Pride's defence

"I said no, and that's final!" replied Lenny sternly. "And I'm not coming down until you all leave!"

Stubbornly, Lenny did just that as the hours went by, and with the crowd growing bigger, Lenny remained perched on one of the beanstalk's giant stalks.

"How long are you going to keep this all up?" asked Leo.

"As long as I have to," replied Lenny. "These are my beans and I'm not letting any of you greedy vultures anywhere near them."

"What's so special about those beans that you're being so protective over them?" asked Leo.

"For the last time, they're my beans and I choose what to do with them, and I choose to keep them all," protested Lenny.

"What's going on here?" yelled a voice from behind the crowd.

The whole crowd instantly turned around and, to their extreme delight and to Lenny's misfortune, bursting through the crowd, pushing everyone out of the way, were Billy the Bison and Bruno the Buffalo.

"Wow, would you look at that, Bruno," said Billy ecstatically.

"I'm looking, Billy, I'm looking," replied Bruno, just as amazed as Billy.

"Where did that come from?" Billy asked.

"Lenny planted it; apparently, he had some magic beans," answered Eric.

"Magic beans?" replied Billy, puzzled.

"That's what he said, and today it was full of bean pods" said Eric. "He's been up there all day picking them."

"We offered our help but he refused," said George.

"Yeah, and he was very rude to Barbra," added Philip "wasn't he, Barbra?"

Barbra, too upset to speak, just nodded a reply before again bursting into tears, which again incited the crowd.

"He won't even share any of his beans," said George, "even to his friends."

"He must have picked thousands of them and he won't even give us one," said Eric.

"Well, we'll see about that," replied Billy, making his way into Lenny's garden, followed by Bruno.

"Stop right there!" said Lenny bravely.

"Or what?" said Billy sternly, not perturbed by Lenny.

"Yeah, what are you going to do about it?" yelled Bruno angrily.

"Nothing, I just don't need any help; I've finished now," replied Lenny hoping to calm them down.

"Then we want some of your beans; we hear that you've picked thousands of them," said Billy.

"I haven't got that many," Lenny lied.

"That's a lie," protested Leo, "you've got sackloads of them."

"Yeah, he's right!" yelled the crowd.

"Right, come down right now and share your beans, or we'll force you down," warned Billy

"No I won't!" replied Lenny.

"Right – don't say we didn't warn you..." said Billy.

After that Billy and Bruno grabbed the beanstalk and began to shake it violently in an attempt to force Lenny to come down.

"Stop, I'm going to fall..." pleaded Lenny, trying desperately to cling on whilst also trying to hold onto the sack.

Billy and Bruno ignored Lenny's pleas and continued to shake the beanstalk with more force; this, in turn, caused him to lose grip and, to prevent himself from falling, he loosened his hold on the sack, causing it to slip from his grasp. Fortunately he managed to grab it before it fell to the ground, but not before some bean pods had fallen out, causing the crowd to surge forward into Lenny's garden to catch the falling prize. Billy and Bruno were the first to catch some (well, no-one dared until they had caught their fill); then there was a mad rush to grab the remainder, driven by the animals' thought of maybe having their own giant beanstalk. Lenny held the sack firmly, in fear that any more might fall, but it was really the fear that, once they opened the pods, they would find the gold beans, and that would spell trouble. That was exactly what happened.

"I'm rich!" yelled Billy after finding the gold bean before frantically opening the other pods.

"Me too!" replied Bruno, who had already opened his pods, and was grinning ecstatically over his gold beans.

"We're rich, we're rich!" sang Billy and Bruno together as they danced around the beanstalk.

Almost immediately, those who had pods frantically opened them, also finding gold beans. Driven by greed and envy, the rest of the crowd stormed the beanstalk and began to shake it; others even began to climb it. Lenny tried his best to hold on but, while holding the sack, it was becoming too difficult, and he had to let go. The minute the sack hit the ground, there was a frenzy of animals fighting to get as many pods as possible. Soon fights broke out as some tried to steal from others and, as usual, Billy and Bruno were in the thick of it.

Lenny, filled with anger from dropping the sack, watched from above the mass brawl taking place beneath him.

"There's more!" shouted Barbra. "I said, there's more!" she shouted louder, to get their attention.

The crowd stopped to face Barbra.

"Where?" asked Billy, angrily.

"In Lenny's house," replied Barbra, grinning uncontrollably.

"That's right," added George, "he's got sackloads in there."

"That's not true," roared Lenny, but it did not stop the crowd besieging his house.

Lenny quickly began to climb down the beanstalk in his attempt to save his beans. He entered his house through his bedroom window, ran down the stairs, grabbed an axe and stood defensively in front of his sacks, as his front door was about to give in under the weight of the crowd of animals eager to get in. It was then that Lenny realised that, even though he had an axe, he was no match for the crowd outside, so he decided to cause a distraction by cutting down the beanstalk. He managed to make his way down the beanstalk without anyone noticing him, as they were too occupied in trying to break down the door. With one huge swing with the axe, he hit the beanstalk with such force that the axe went a third of the way through. The crowd stopped instantly and faced Lenny, who was preparing for a second, and what would probably be the final, swing at the beanstalk.

"Stop! Are you mad?" exclaimed Eric. "It could fall on our house!"

"Never mind that; it could fall on us!" replied Pete the Panther.

"Yeah, you're right; we all could be crushed!" screamed Olivia the Ostrich.

Suddenly, there was great panic, as they all tried desperately to flee through Lenny's garden gate, causing the whole fence to give way to the stampede. The axe struck the beanstalk with another hard hit, and this time it was enough to send it over.

"Timber!" roared Lenny as all the hysterical animals

just managed to escape before the beanstalk hit the ground, missing Lenny's house and, to their great relief, Eric and George's house as well. The beanstalk slowly began to wither away, to the amazement of the animals and – to their great disappointment – the pods, the beans, and not to mention the gold ones, completely disappeared.

"What have you done, you crazy lion?" screamed Billy in disappointment of his loss.

"Kill him!" yelled Bruno.

"Yes, kill him!" implored Barbra.

The whole crowd was about to charge but, fortunately for poor Lenny, Leo jumped in front of the crowd to stop them.

"Wait!" yelled Leo, to the much-relieved Lenny, who stood in his garden, preparing to defend himself with his axe."Why should we?" replied Billy angrily.

"Yeah, why should we?" said the crowd.

"We've lost our beans because of him," added Chris the Cheetah

"Yeah," said the crowd.

"That's true, but so has he," replied Leo.

"We don't care about him, he deserves it, the way he treated me," argued Barbra.

"Yeah, she's right," said Philip.

"You may be right, Barbra, but he doesn't deserve this,"

said Leo.

"He's right, everyone," said Larry the Lion, agreeing with Leo.

"That's rubbish; he deserves all he gets," replied Barbra angrily.

"Come on, Barbra, because he was rude to you? I'm sure he had his reasons," pleaded Leo.

"Have you forgotten he was rude to you too?" said Barbra.

"Yeah," replied Eric and George together.

"I know he was, but I think we're being too harsh," said Leo.

"I've had enough of all this, kill him, I say kill him!" interrupted Billy, inciting the crowd again.

"Yeah, kill him!" yelled the crowd.

"No wait, this isn't right," pleaded Leo.

"Don't worry, Leo; we're not going to kill him, we're just going to give him a good beating, that's all," replied Billy.

"Yeah, Billy and I do love a bit of a scrap, but we're not murderers," said Bruno honestly, "and I'm sure that goes for the rest of them..."

"Yeah," agreed the crowd.

"I'm glad to hear it," said Leo, relieved, "but he doesn't

even deserve a beating too."

"No way!" replied the crowd.

"Look... yes, Lenny did upset some of us because of his greed for wealth, but we're not completely innocent. Don't forget that we were prepared to break into poor Lenny's house to steal his beans because of our greed too. So we became exactly like Lenny. So, if anyone needs a beating, it's us too!" explained Leo.

"If he had shared the beans in the first place, all this would not have happened," replied Billy.

"That may be the case, but it still does not excuse our behaviour," said Leo.

There was a short silence while they waited for Billy and Bruno to come to a decision.

"Leo, you're right, but he'd better not step out of line," replied Billy, after talking with Bruno.

The crowd slowly dispersed as soon as Billy and Bruno left, leaving Lenny to deal with the remains of the now-shrivelled-up beanstalk, which looked more like a giant twig.

Things took a while to get back to normal with everyone ignoring Lenny for a while, except for Leo, Larry, Luther and Lester, who were more forgiving. As for the rest of the jungle animals, they were less forgiving, despite Lenny's apologies. Eventually, as the weeks went by, it slowly became forgotten. Eric and George continued to lap up the sun on their lawn. Barbra and Philip became very good friends, until he upset her by turning up late when she had invited him for dinner. It would have been fine if it was a few hours, but he arrived a day later to face a very angry baboon. Billy and Bruno spent many days dreaming of what it would have been like if they had really become rich.

The End

....

As for Lenny, he learnt another valuable lesson he would never forget. Although it is nice to be rich, it is also important to have good friends. His greed for wealth had caused him to become very cruel, and had almost lost him the friends who were dear to him. He also learnt that things would have been different if he had shared the beans with everyone, since there were plenty to go around. Fortunately for Lenny, he did have good friends, despite having treated them badly, and was very glad; despite losing his riches, he still had his good friends.

It is God who entrust us with wealth and we must be wise in how we use it and not let it control us. Jesus warns us that we cannot serve both God and money, and that we should serve God by using our wealth for his kingdom and to help those in need. Money gives us a false sense of security, but we should look to God to provide for our needs. Just like Lenny, we could get wealth and soon lose it as quickly as it took to get it. But God will always take care of us and, as Lenny found out, the right friendships are with those who don't care how much money you have and forgive you when you have made mistakes.

Lastly, it is also wrong to bully anyone, just because you are bigger or stronger than them. Billy and Bruno's behaviour is not what God expects from us. As he is love, we too must do the same and never mistreat anyone.

Matthew 6:24, Hebrews 13:5, 1 Timothy 6:10, Romans 8:39, Proverbs 17:9.

THE GREAT WORLD ANIMAL RACE

Ever since my dad took me to see my first Great World Animal Race, I have been a huge fan, and have never missed one since. But out of all the races I've seen (and I've many great races), I will never forget the race that shocked the world and is still talked about to this very day.

The Karoomba jungle was making history as it was hosting, for the first time, the Great World Animal Race. There was a feel-good factor about the place as animals from around the world flocked into the Karoomba, especially into Leo's fruit juice parlour. It was so full inside that many had to stand outside. Thankfully Leo, Larry, Luther, Lester and Lenny were all there to give their friend a helping hand by going around serving the thirsty spectators in return for free drinks all day.

"If it continues at this rate, Leo, you'll be out of drinks before the evening," said Lenny, placing a tray load of empty glasses onto the counter.

"Don't worry. Lenny, I anticipated it would be like this, so I've brought in a few extra barrels," replied Leo, passing the tray over to his assistant, Betty the Bobcat.

When Leo heard that the Karoomba jungle was to host the Great World Animal Race, he danced around his parlour with excitement at the prospect of making a very handsome profit, and right he was, having filled three money boxes already.

"I should have known," said Lenny, wiping the sweat from his forehead. "You've always been one for making the most of an opportunity to make more money.

"Yeah, I know," bragged Leo, looking at the almost full fourth money box. "Something I learnt from my father."

"He sure did have a way with money, your father," replied Lenny.

"He did… and he always made sure he gave some to the poor, too," replied Leo.

It was a mild day – ideal weather for the race – which was soon about to start. A stand (to sit the Mayor. the four Karoomba Great World Animal Race committee members, the president of the Great World Animal Race Association and several VIP guests) was built next to the starting line. A gazebo, too, was set up for them all to have lunch while the race was underway.

George the Giraffe and Eric the Elephant, who were literally the first there, had set up camp, placing their recliners and cool box right at the front of the track, in the best possible place.

"It's going to be a great turnout, I think," said George, looking around at the animals that had already turned up.

"Let's hope the race is a good one," replied Eric, "and I hope it won't be like the one two years back – remember? The one in the Redski Jungle, where no-one finished the race?"

"I do! Oh Goodness, I hope not!" wished George.

A trumpet signalled attention for all the spectators who had lined up along either side of the track, and a podium was placed in the middle of the starting line, for the president of the Great World Animal Race Association, Reginald the Rhino. Stepping up towards the podium first was Arnold the Antelope, the Great World Animal Race committee leader of the Karoomba section, who was responsible for organising the race.

"Felines, Canines, Apes, Reptiles, Rodents, Birds, Marsupials, Hooveds and other kinds of animals, I welcome you to the Karoomba jungle for this great annual event. I want to say it's a great privilege and honour to host the Great World Animal Race in the Karoomba. As it's the jungle's first time, I hope that it will be a memorable one. Now, before I invite the President of the G.W.A.R.A. (Great World Animal Race Association), I welcome our very own honourable mayor, Toby the Tiger, who would like to say something."

"I would like to say that it is a privilege to have the Great World Animal Race here in the Karoomba, and that the committee have done a wonderful job in their preparations," said the mayor. "Now, before I hand over the podium, I want to wish all the contestants all the best… and may the best animal win." The crowd cheered loudly. "Now I want you all to stand and welcome Reginald, the president of the Great World Animal Race Association."

There was a great sound of clapping, screeching, roaring, howling and neighing as Reginald the Rhino climbed the podium steps.

"Welcome, welcome, everybody, to the seventeenth Great World Animal Race. First, I would also like to applaud the Karoomba jungle committee for their excellent preparations for this great event. I also want to thank all the animals who helped in the preparations, and also, all the animals who have travelled from all over the world to watch this race."

There was a huge cheer from all the spectators before Reginald continued:

"Now I, Reginald, president of the G.W.A.R.A., declare that the seventeenth Great World Animal Race… is open!"

The crowd cheered even more loudly when Reginald left the podium, and the opening ceremony began with the sound of drums from the Chimps Aloud band, led by Charlie the Chimpanzee. This was then followed by a group of ballerina ostriches who performed a very entertaining dance routine. The spectators cheered as they were entertained by acrobats, singing, and a parade of animals, all dressed in impressive, colourful costumes.

After over an hour of exhilarating entertainment, the ceremony finally drew to an end. Patricia the Penguin, committee member, approached the podium and politely gestured the crowd to be silent, so that she could announce the competitors for this year's race."Everybody please stand and welcome our first competitor. Running in lane one and attending his fourth Great World Animal Race: Karoomba Jungle's very own Chris the Cheetah."

The majority of the spectators cheered with excitement as Chris approached the track, waving to his fans.

"In lane two, representing the Atokis forest, running in his second Great World Animal Race: Harold the Hare."Harold received cheers as he made his way to lane two.

"In lane three, being his second appearance, from the Catoomos plains, Trevor the Tortoise."

Trevor received a loud reception from almost all of the spectators who had remembered his heroic race last year, when he finished ahead of Harold the Hare.

"In lane four: Saroomba jungle's very own Edward the Elk, in his third Great World Animal Race."

More cheers from the crowd, mainly from Saroomba spectators.

"Representing Redski Forest, and running in lane five, competing in his first ever Great World Animal Race: Boris the Badger.""Go, go, Boris!" cheered the Redski spectators.

"In lane six, from the Zolos grassland and running his first race: Curtis the Coyote."

"We love you, Curtis, we do... we love Curtis, we do... we love Curtis, we do... oh, Curtis, we love you!" sang the Zolos spectators."In lane seven, in her second Great World Animal Race, running for Wombot grassland: Wilma the Wallaby.

"Hooray, hooray for Wilma!" yelled the Wombot spectators.

"In lane eight, from the Mambos savannah, running her third Great World Animal Race and the reigning champion: Georgina the Gazelle!""We are the champions, we are the champions!" sang the Mambos spectators.

"In lane nine, all the way from Artok Forest in his first Great World Animal Race, Wilson the wolf."

"Wilson, Wilson, Wilson, Wilson!" chanted the Artok spectators.

"And finally, in lane ten, from the Sassoon plains and running in his third Great World Animal Race: Elliot the Emu."

Cheers and chanting followed from the Sassoon spectators as the final competitor took up his position on the track.

"Welcome to all the qualifiers of the seventeenth Great World Animal Race. I wish you all the best as you all compete for the chance to become world champion!" said Patricia. "Please all stand once again for our committee leader."

Arnold took to the podium once more to start the race as the competitors donned their tracksuits. "Welcome, all runners; please will you make your way to your starting blocks? The lanes end after one hundred yards; after that, follow the red flags until you return back here to the finish line. There is a checkpoint at every half-mile where you can grab some refreshments," explained Arnold. "Now... are you all ready?"

The runners all waved a reply, and positioned themselves at the starting blocks, waiting for Arnold to start the two-and-a-half mile race.

"Ready...steady... go!" commanded Arnold, and all ten competitors began the race.

Chris the Cheetah was first to leave the blocks as he was off in a flash, sending the Karoomba spectators into hysterical cheering. He was followed by Georgina the Gazelle, Wilson the Wolf, Curtis the Coyote, Elliot the Emu, Wilma the Wallaby, Edward the Elk, Harold the Hare, Boris the Badger and, lastly, Trevor the Tortoise, who had only reached a couple of metres when the others had disappeared from view.

Most of the spectators went off to amuse themselves amongst the variety of stalls that the committee had set up. They sold all sorts – from food to clothing to souvenirs – and there were even games. The rest either went straight to Leo's parlour or chose to see how long it would take for Trevor to disappear from view. The committee's hired workers were busy repositioning the stand so that it could face the runners as they approached the finishing line. The mayor, committee, president and guests all made their way to the gazebo for a highly exquisite lunch, all paid for by the one-and-only taxpayer.

"Here, Georgie-boy, try some of this," said Eric, passing George a glass of a green-coloured liquid.

"What is it?" replied George, looking at it sceptically.

"It's my new drink I've invented!" said Eric, grinning excitedly.

"What's in it?" George replied, taking a sniff.

"Trust me, you'll like it," reassured Eric.

"Mmmm, this is great!" said George, licking his lips before taking a second gulp.

"Like some more?" laughed Eric.

"Yes please," replied George handing back the now empty glass. "What's it made of?"

"Some exotic fruit and spices... which I don't wish to reveal," explained Eric.

"Can't say I blame you," replied George. "You should let Leo try it; maybe he might sell it in his parlour, just like your tropical fruit drink."

"That's the plan, Georgie-boy, that's the plan."

While Eric and George indulged joyfully in the delightful invention, Chris had reached the first checkpoint, with Wilma and Georgina close behind. A gap of two minutes separated Wilson, Elliot and Edward, who were pacing themselves to retain their energy. Harold and Boris were about five minutes from the checkpoint while Curtis was taking his time a minute behind them. As for Trevor, he was only just completing a third of the first half-mile.Now, there was a reason why Curtis was taking his time, for he was very determined to win the race: so determined, in fact, that he was prepared to cheat. Secretly, Curtis (with the help of his accomplices, two very cunning weasels, Wesley and Wallace) had devised a plan that would help him win the race by forcing the other competitors out.

Meanwhile, back at Leo's fruit juice parlour, Lenny, Larry, Luther and Lester were relieved that it had quietened down a little, and jumped at the chance for a well-deserved rest. They sat outside and watched the spectators trying in vain to win prizes at the various games the stalls had to offer.

"Word has it that Chris is still in the lead at the first checkpoint," said Luther.

"It would be great if he wins it," replied Lenny, "but I don't see it."

"Yeah, I agree," said Larry, joining in the conversation. "He's maybe the fastest but I don't see him lasting the course."

"Well, you never know," replied Lenny, being optimistic.

"I personally think Wilma's going to win this year," said Luther.

"Georgina's looking strong again this year, though," replied Lester.

"I think it's going to be a close call between Georgina and Elliot," said Lenny.

"Elliot?" laughed Luther. "That old bird won't last two miles!"

"Chris has a good chance, but Larry's right, I can't see him lasting. It would be great if he does, but Georgina's fast and has the stamina to last the course," said Lester.

"Yeah, you're right, Lester; I think the closest one to give her a hard time would be Chris... or even Wilson," replied Lenny.

"Wilson?" exclaimed Larry, Luther and Lester together.

"I don't care who wins it, just as long as it isn't a dog!" said Luther.

"Hear, hear," replied the rest, as they raised their glasses in agreement.

Back to the race and all the competitors had long passed the first checkpoint, apart from Trevor, of course, who was not even halfway. Chris was still in first place with Georgina in second and Wilma in third. The gap between the rest had increased, with Elliot in fourth, then a two-minute gap separated Wilson in fifth. Edward had dropped into seventh as Harold had overtaken him to take sixth position. Five minutes behind Edward, in eighth, was Boris... and Curtis, in ninth, was taking his time, knowing that – if his plan succeeded – he was definitely going to win.

Meanwhile, at the finishing line, George and Eric had eaten and drunk everything they had brought with them.

"What are we going to eat now? I'm still hungry," asked Eric patting his stomach.

"Me too," replied George. "I knew we should have packed more stuff."

"No point worrying about that now; what are we going to do?" asked a frustrated Eric.

"How should I know; you're the one with the bright ideas," replied George.

"Why don't you think of something for a change?" said Eric sternly.

"Why should I? That's your job," replied George.

"Since when?" protested Eric.

"Since you came up with all the ideas: that's when!" answered George.

"You're right, Georgie-boy; I think I have one right now," replied Eric, looking at the waiter coming out of the VIP gazebo with a bag of rubbish. "Get ready, Georgie-boy, for some posh nosh."

"I'm on your wavelength, Eric," said George, seeing

Eric's point of view.

"I say, young Baboon, I say, can I have your attention?" called out Eric.

"What? I'm busy," replied the Baboon rudely.

"I won't keep you, I was wondering if there was any food left over?" asked Eric.

"Yeah, loads," replied the Baboon, "what's it to you?"

"You couldn't be a nice chap and, er, bring some out for us, could you?" asked Eric politely.

"No," answered the Baboon bluntly.

"Why not? It's only going to waste," interrupted George.

"Please, George, let me handle this," said Eric, calming George down. "If it's going to be thrown away, it might as well be put to good use," he added politely.

"I thought it had already served its purpose," replied the waiter.

"Well it could serve another purpose by saving two animals from starvation," replied Eric.

"You both look well-fed to me," said the waiter. "Especially you," he added, referring to Eric, before heading back into the gazebo.

"Well, don't say I didn't try," said Eric glumly.

"Well, it looks like it's the food in Leo's bar then,"

replied George, unenthusiastically.

"You can forget that, Georgie-boy; it looks like the waiter's come through for us," said Eric, overjoyed, when the waiter returned with a bag full of food.

"You guys might as well put this food to some good use, since it will probably end up being thrown away," replied the waiter, having a change of heart.

"Thank you, thank you!" replied Eric, expressing his gratitude as he and George danced around with joy.

Back to the race and, as they passed the second checkpoint, Chris was still leading the pack, but Georgina, in second place, was right behind him, followed by Wilma, Elliot, Edward, Harold, Boris, Curtis and Trevor. Soon some of them grew tired and, by the time they reached the third checkpoint, the race order was changing constantly. Georgina had taken the lead by a two-minute gap, with Wilma in second and Wilson in third. Chris had slipped down to fourth place with Edward and Elliot close behind. Harold, Boris and Curtis were almost at the third checkpoint, and, finally, Trevor was approaching the first checkpoint at last.

At the fourth checkpoint, Wesley and Wallace were busily preparing to execute their cunning plan. They hoped to distract the two reindeer at the refreshment stand long enough for them to lace the water with sleeping powder without being spotted. They managed to crawl towards a bush directly behind them and, on the count of three, Wesley chucked a hornets' nest over the bush. It landed right at the reindeers' feet, breaking in half and releasing loads of angry hornets. They ran for their lives with the hornets in hot pursuit, allowing the two weasels to sabotage all the drinks. The reindeer returned several minutes later, after jumping into a lake to escape the swarm, and were none the wiser that the drinks had been spiked.

Georgina was the first to reach the fourth check point grabbing a cup of water as she ran past, followed by Wilson, Edward, Wilma, Chris, Elliot, Harold, and Boris, each of them taking a cup of water.

"Mission accomplished," whispered Wallace to Wesley as they watched from behind the bush.

"Yeah, Curtis will be pleased," Wesley replied.

"We'd better go and wait for him at the rendezvous point," said Wallace, as both weasels crawled away until they were out of sight.It did not take long for the sleeping powder to take effect, as one by one the animals were all overwhelmed by tiredness, until they could run no more; they found a place to sit down and, before long, they fell fast asleep. When Curtis jogged past the sleeping runners, he was filled with joy, and sang to himself all the way to the rendezvous point.

"The race is mine, oh, it's mine!" sang a highly jubilant Curtis, who knew that the only one left who could possibly beat him was Trevor, and the chances of that were very slim indeed.

"Champion-ey, champion-ey, you're the champion..."

Wesley and Wallace chanted merrily together.

"Thank you, thank you," replied Curtis, bowing. "Now make yourselves scarce before anyone sees us together and they work out that you put sleeping powder in the water. Now be on your way, I've got a race to win."

Back at the finishing line, the mayor, committee, president of the G.W.A.R.A. and guests were all seated in the stands, waiting for the race leader to appear. Finally, Curtis crossed the line to receive a huge welcome mixture of applause, cheers and chanting. Curtis relished the moment immensely as he danced around in front of his highly jubilant fans.   After an hour since Curtis had finished the race, everyone was wondering about the other competitors who still had not shown up. Soon many of the spectators were getting restless and began to voice their opinions. It was then that Reginald requested that Ricardo the Raven look for the missing competitors.

While all the excitement was going on at the finishing line, Trevor had arrived at the fourth checkpoint to find no one there to give him water. Disappointed, he continued and eventually passed Boris, then – several yards further – he met Harold.

"Hah! You haven't learnt from the last time!" said Trevor quietly to the hare, who was sleeping peacefully against a rock.

Meanwhile, Ricardo returned to inform the committee of what had happened to all the runners.

Reginald stood on the podium and spoke. "We have just learned that the other competitors are unable to finish the race, so – since Curtis the Coyote is the only one to finish the race and was first to pass the finish line – I declare Curtis, of the Zolos grasslands, winner of this year's Great World Animal Race."

"Hooray, hooray!" shouted the Zolos spectators as Curtis stepped onto the winners' podium to receive the trophy.

"He's a cheat!" yelled someone, silencing the crowd.

"Who said that?" replied Arnold. "Show yourself."

From amongst the crowd of spectators stepped a meerkat. "I did."

"What is your name?" asked Arnold.

"My name is Michael," replied the meerkat.

"What evidence have you got that Curtis cheated?" asked Arnold.

"We overheard him bragging about it to his two friends," replied Michael.

"Do you have proof of this?" asked Arnold.

"My brothers and sisters saw everything..." answered Michael.

At that moment, several other meerkats appeared, all with the same accusation against Curtis.

"Curtis, is this true?" asked Reginald taking over from

Arnold.

"It's all lies! Lies, I tell you!" said Curtis in his defence.

"You're the one who's lying – you cheated: you made them put sleeping powder in the refreshments!" replied Michael.

"Let's just take it easy before things get out of hand. Now, Michael, tell me exactly what you saw," said Reginald, interrupting before an argument broke out.

"We were all making our way towards the finishing line when we saw runner after runner fast asleep. We thought it was strange for them all to be asleep, so we tried to wake them up, but it was pointless. We were continuing on our way when we heard Curtis singing, so we decided to follow him. We saw Curtis with two friends celebrating the fact that his plan had succeeded.""That's all nonsense. I won this race fair and square," pleaded Curtis.

There was a short pause while Reginald and the committee members discussed what to do next.

"The committee members and I have decided that we shall not award any prize until there is an investigation into these allegations," said Reginald. "In the meantime, until the investigators get to the bottom of this, can you all please be patient?"

"I don't believe you're going to believe a bunch of meerkats," protested Curtis.

"I'm sorry Curtis, we cannot ignore this serious accusation, plus it all looks suspicious to me with you being the only one to finish the race," replied Reginald before making his way into the gazebo.

The crowd remained subdued, except for the odd whisper, which made Curtis very uncomfortable. The thought of a quick getaway did cross his mind, but the prospect of becoming Great World Animal Race champion was far too great to give up. "Looks like we'll be here for a while," said George.

"Yeah, I know, and we have nothing to eat or drink," replied Eric glumly.

"Tell me about it," agreed George.

"Trust a coyote to cheat," said Eric.

"Steady on, Eric, we don't know that for sure," replied George.

"Come on, George, look at him, there's guilt written all over his face," said Eric.

"I suppose you're right, but you know what they say, 'innocent until proven guilty' and all..." said George.

"Yeah, I agree, but think about it, Georgie-boy, isn't it strange that Curtis is the only one to finish the race?" said Eric."You might have a point," replied George.

"You see? I'm right!" said Eric.

"Well, let's not judge him until the investigations are over..." said George.

After a couple of hours of waiting patiently a small

section of the crowd began to cheer loudly and, to everyone's surprise, approaching the finishing line very slowly was Trevor the Tortoise. Soon all the spectators (well, apart from the Zolos) began to give him a standing ovation. Trevor, who had no idea of what had happened, crossed the line thinking he had finished in last place, and was thrilled to hear that he had finished second.

Shortly after Trevor had finished the race, the investigators returned. They followed Reginald and the committee into the gazebo to share what they had found. Frederick the Fox, who had led the investigations, began to read out the report.

"After our thorough investigations, we thought we were not going to find any evidence of foul play by any of the competitors. However, as we were finishing near the last checkpoint, we stopped two weasels. When we confronted them, and told them if they did not co-operate they would face serious consequences, they quickly told us what they had done and that Curtis had planned it all. Here is some of the sleeping powder they used to spike their drinks," he finished, holding up a small packet.

"Right, that's all we need. We'd better make the announcement," replied Reginald.

Reginald stepped up to the podium and called for everyone's attention. The crowd instantly went quiet, eagerly waiting for the verdict.

"Following the investigations and with evidence and a confession, I hereby disqualify Curtis for cheating in order to win the race," said Reginald.

"What! That's not true; I didn't cheat!" exclaimed Curtis.

"Do you know a Wallace and Wesley?" asked Reginald.

"No, I've never met them," replied Curtis, lying. "Well according to the signed confession of Wallace and Wesley Weasel, they say that you instructed them to spike the refreshments with sleeping powder," replied Reginald.

"Those weasels are liars!" yelled Curtis.

"Not once did I, or anyone else, ever mention that they were weasels; how did you know?" said Reginald.

"I... err... err..." replied Curtis, before making a run for it.

"Well, I now have no other choice than to announce that the new Great World Animal Race winner is... Trevor!" said Reginald. There was a huge roar from the crowd of spectators as Trevor slowly made his way towards the winner's podium to collect his trophy. No-one had anticipated that a tortoise would win the Great World Animal Race, especially with the likes of a cheetah and a gazelle competing.

The closing ceremony shortly followed with once again the Chimps Aloud band supplying the music, as the spectators watched a performance by the Flamingo School of Dance. During the celebrations, Wilma crossed the finishing line to claim second place, and was shortly followed by Chris, Edward, Georgina, Wilson, Elliot, Boris and, in last place, a very distraught Harold, especially distraught when he found out that Trevor had won the race.

Finally, and with much relief to the committee, this year's Great World Animal Race was over until next year, as the spectators slowly made their way home. No-one ever saw Curtis again, who was issued a lifetime ban from ever competing in another Great World Animal Race. Curtis did not realise the consequences of his actions: that, if you keep on cheating and being dishonest, you will eventually be found out. If Curtis was honest, and did not cheat, he would have certainly not have been humiliated and have his name ruined by his actions. Now, instead of running the race honestly and possibly winning, everyone will remember him as the coyote that cheated. Trevor, on the other hand, never thought he would win. No-one gave him a chance. Trevor finishing the race was an achievement in itself, but to go on and win was a dream come true. Trevor's achievement shows that, when you persevere in something you truly believe in, you will achieve things much higher than what you sent out to do to begin with. Trevor became a hero when he returned home and was given the freedom of the Catoomos plains. Trevor did not repeat his achievement of the previous year at the Great World Animal Race the following year, which was held in the Wombot grasslands, but the standing ovation he received was more than enough for him. Harold finally finished ahead of Trevor, in ninth place, to ease the haunting memory of Trevor's triumph the year before. Georgina once again celebrated a win and, as for Eric's new drink, it was not as popular as he had hoped and, after a month, Leo had no other choice than to stop selling it at his parlour. This did not discourage him one bit, and he promised to invent another one soon, to the delight of George.

The End

....

Lying, cheating and dishonesty are all things that do not please God. We may be able to hide things from people, but we can never hide anything from God, who sees everything. We will always please God when we are honest and tell the truth; even if lying will get us out of trouble, we must not do it.Also, if we ask God for help, and trust in His divine strength to help us, we will not need to cheat to achieve anything or try to rely on our own strength and understanding. God is always willing to help us, as long as we trust in him, and sometimes the way he helps us may not be the way we expect. We just have to believe and trust that his ways are far better for us.

Colossians 3:9, Proverbs 12:22, Psalms 37:37, Proverbs 3:5, Philippians 4:13.

....

THE HOLES

Who would have thought that holes in the ground would lead to one of the greatest adventure that some of the jungle inhabitants have ever witnessed? Add action, betrayal, and Leo, George and Eric in the mix and you will agree. Well, let me not delay a second more. Sit back, relax, and enjoy the ride.

Rain fell heavily upon the Karoomba jungle, keeping most of the animals indoors. A bored and frustrated Eric the Elephant and George the Giraffe watched from their bedroom windows for the rain to stop.

"Looks like the rain's not going to end," said Eric glumly, looking at the sky from his bedroom window.

"It's a shame. I could have done with an afternoon on the lawn," replied George, looking up at the sky as well.

"Me too," said Eric. "What are we going to do now? I'm bored."

"There's nothing we can do but wait for the rain to

stop," replied George.

"I wonder what he's doing?" said Eric, looking over at Lenny's house.

"I can only think of one thing," replied George confidently.

"Sleeping," answered both Eric and George at the same time.

Eric and George were right; Lenny the Lion was in bed doing the things he loved most, sleeping and dreaming of eating. This time he was dreaming that he was trapped in a room made of marshmallows and toffee, and the only way out was to eat his way out.

"I've got an idea how we can amuse ourselves," said Eric.

"Yeah? Tell me more," replied George excitedly.

"Samuel the Squirrel gave me a bag full of hazelnuts. I thought we could throw some through Lenny's window, since it's slightly open," said Eric.

"That's a great idea, Eric!" replied George. "Let's see who can get the most nuts through the gap in Lenny's window."

"Yes, let's!" said Eric with a huge smile.

After using a broom to pass George a bag of nuts, they began to aim for Lenny's window. After a several misses, they were soon getting their missiles through the open window and, before long, some were hitting the target: Lenny. "That's four-two to me!" yelled George with excitement as his nut disappeared through Lenny's bedroom window.

The nut hit Lenny hard on the forehead, waking him abruptly from his entertaining dream.

"That's enough, you two; you're disturbing my quiet time!" roared Lenny from his bedroom window.

"Oh, come on, Lenny, you're spoiling our fun!" replied Eric.

"I don't see the fun in it, somehow," said Lenny rubbing his forehead.

"What are we going to do now?" said George.

"I'm sure if both of you put what little minds you have together you'll think of something," replied Lenny sarcastically.

"What else can we do? In case you haven't noticed, it's not exactly a nice day," said Eric.

"Maybe you could do a bit of gardening," Lenny joked, pointing down at Eric's garden.

Eric and George both looked down and were surprised they had not noticed it before now.

"Where did those come from?" said a bewildered Eric, looking at three large holes, which were rapidly filling up with water in the middle of his garden."I don't know, perhaps some meteors fell during the night?" replied George, who was just as baffled as his neighbour.

It rained throughout the rest of the day and continued into the night as Eric and George eventually faced up to staying home, to their disappointment. George did not sleep well during the night as he kept wondering about the mysterious holes in Eric's garden. The next morning he was welcomed by a bright, sunny, cloudless day, bringing relief to the inhabitants of the Karoomba jungle, especially Eric and George. With only a few hours sleep, George emerged from his front door to find Eric already there, leaning over his garden fence.

"Morning, Georgie-boy," said Eric.

"Morning," George replied with a yawn.

"Didn't get much sleep, I take it?" replied Eric.

"Yeah; couldn't help wondering about those holes," said George.

"Well, whoever's responsible for making the holes has taken a fancy to your garden," replied Eric, pointing to half a dozen freshly-dug holes in George's garden.

"Blimey, Eric, who could be doing this?" replied George.

"It beats me, but I know now it's not meteors," said Eric.

"Do you think it's those moles from down the road?" said George.

"Nah, it can't be them, they're too big to be mole holes," said Eric.

"Yeah you're right there, even too big to be rabbit or even meerkat burrows," said George.

"What are you guys doing – digging for oil?" Lenny yelled from his bedroom window.

"We thought we could do a bit of landscape gardening," replied Eric sarcastically.

"Now, jokes aside, what's with the holes?" asked Lenny curiously.

"Your guess is as good as ours," replied Eric. "We don't know where they've come from. Yesterday they appeared in my garden and today in George's."

"That's strange, very strange," replied Lenny. "It could be either a freak of nature or an overenthusiastic mole."

"It could be one of those mysteries that will never be solved," said Eric.

"Who knows? Maybe one day it will be," said Lenny.

As usual, everyone began to hear about the mysterious holes in Eric and George's garden, and, over the next couple of days, more holes began to appear all over the jungle, causing such concern to the animals that they decided to hold a meeting. Many animals made an appearance and, after a long night of discussions, they finally agreed to have a patrol during the night in the hope of catching whoever was making the holes. It was also reluctantly agreed that, since the holes first appeared in George and Eric's garden, they should be the first to patrol the jungle. The following night, George waited patiently for Eric to emerge from his house so that they could begin their night patrol. After waiting for several minutes he decided to knock on his door. He started gently at first and, when he did not get a response, he began to knock loudly and eventually resorted to banging.

"Will you stop that racket, I'm trying to sleep!" yelled Lenny, who had been woken by the continual banging. "Sorry Lenny, I'm trying to wake up Eric," replied George apologetically. "We're supposed to start the patrol, but he's only gone and overslept."

"Leave him; you know Eric, he'll sleep through an earthquake," said Lenny.

"I know, but I have to wake him; I don't fancy patrolling the jungle on my own!" said George desperately.

"I tell you what; since I'm awake, I'll come with you," said Lenny.

"Oh, thanks, Lenny, you're a star!" replied a jubilant George.

"Well, I might as well, since you've woken me..." said Lenny.

Lenny and George patrolled the jungle for almost all of the night without finding one freshly-dug hole or even catching the perpetrator red-handed. Apart from the tree frogs' mating calls and the odd nocturnal animal, Lenny and George were the only animals roaming the jungle at night. Lenny hinted that he was getting tired, and George didn't hesitate to take a rest. Lenny jumped at the idea and found a log for them both to sit on.

"This is a waste of time; we must have walked for miles," complained George.

"Well, I don't know about you, but I'm calling it a night" said Lenny.

"I can't say I disagree," replied George.

At that moment they heard footsteps heading quickly towards them, and as fear gripped George, he grabbed Lenny for some sort of protection.

"It's the phantom hole-maker; we're going to die!" shrieked George.

"Calm down George, it's probably Eric coming to find us." replied Lenny, reassuring a frightened George.

"But it sounds like there's loads of them coming towards us!" said George hysterically.

"Well, Eric's kind of big..." replied Lenny.

Suddenly, out of the vegetation, came a chicken followed by a hen, turkey, duck and goose. "It's falling down, it's falling down!" they all yelled, before disappearing into the jungle

"What's falling down?" said a bemused Lenny.

"Your guess is as good as mine," replied George, shrugging his shoulders.

"This is all pointless; I'm off home, you coming?" said Lenny heading into the jungle.

"Thought you'd never ask," replied George, hurrying to keep up with Lenny.

As they made their way home, they suddenly heard shouts for help. Lenny, without hesitation, went to their aid, with George reluctantly following. They were led straight towards Zed the Zebra's house and were very surprised to see what they saw there.

"What's going on, Zed?" asked Lenny as soon as they arrived.

"Thank goodness you're here! I've caught the hole-digger!" said Zed hysterically.

George and Lenny looked down and, standing in a huge hole, was someone with a white sheet, which Zed had used to catch the culprit.

"You sure?" said Lenny.

"Of course I'm sure, I caught him digging the hole; look, there's his spade," replied Zed.

Zed was right – it did seem that whoever was under the sheet was responsible for digging a huge hole in Zed's garden.

"Did you kill him?" said George, looking at the lifeless body.

"I don't know; I did hit him hard with my broom," said Zed.

"Look, he's moving!" yelled Lenny.

George quickly picked up the spade, Zed took aim with his broom, and Lenny grabbed the end of the sheet.

"On the count of three," said Lenny. "One... two... three!"

Everyone stood gobsmacked when Lenny removed the sheet to reveal who was responsible for digging the holes over the past few days. There, standing as bemused as those who were about to hit him by a broom and a spade, stood Eric the Elephant.

"Eric!" shouted Zed, George and Lenny together.

"What are you guys doing in my bedroom?" replied Eric dozily.

"Your bedroom? You're in Zed's front garden!" said George.

"What am I doing here?" said a puzzled Eric, looking around at his surroundings.

"You tell us," said George.

"I haven't a clue; the last thing I remember was going to bed early so that I could wake up to go on patrol with you, George, and the next thing, I'm standing here looking at you three with an awful headache," explained Eric, rubbing his head.

"Oh, I do apologise for that," said Zed quietly.

"So, basically, for the last few days you have been digging all the holes while you were sleep-walking," said George.

"No, that can't be true, can it?" replied an Eric, who felt slightly embarrassed.

"How do you explain the hole you're standing in then?" said Zed.

"Maybe some aliens abducted him and then dropped him in the hole they had dug," said Lenny chuckling to himself.

"Well, he'd better get those aliens to come back to fill the hole," said Zed, as both he and Lenny laughed at Eric's expense.

"Come on, guys, enough with the jokes," said George in Eric's defence.

"Oh George, where's your sense of humour?" replied Lenny.

"Yeah, it is kind of funny," said George grinning.

"Maybe it's not Eric at all. Maybe it's an alien after all and has taken over Eric's body," said Lenny mockingly.

"Yeah, just like that story I once read. From what I can remember, it was about an invasion of aliens who snatched bodies," replied Zed. "Maybe that's what the holes are for."

Lenny and George looked bemused.

"You know... for those pod-type things?" said Zed. "What the aliens use to make copies of us," explained Zed, as Lenny and George still looked confused. "According to the story, they used a pod-type thing to make a copy of anyone they chose, and those who the aliens had copied hadn't any feelings or emotions…""Ouch!" cried Eric, after Zed hit him on the head again with his broom.

"I take it he's not an alien, then," said Lenny sarcastically,

"No, apparently not," replied Zed, slightly disappointed.

"Guys, when you're finished deciding if I'm an alien or not, I'd like to let you know that I am cold; I have one – no, sorry, two – bumps on my head, a headache, and I am also getting quite hungry; now I could do with some help out of this hole, if you don't mind!" said Eric sternly.

George instantly went to Eric's aid and tried in vain to help him out of the hole; in fact, it was obvious that George was not strong enough, so Lenny had to help. With Lenny's help, Eric was slowly pulled out of the hole, but as they were helping him out, somehow Lenny fell into the hole.

"Hey Lenny, are you alright?" asked George.

"Here, Eric, you've gone and killed Lenny!" said Zed after there was no reply from Lenny.

"I'm alright," replied Lenny. "I think I've found something."

"Is it a pod?" replied Zed.

"It's a sort of metal box, I think," answered Lenny.

"Is it gold?" asked Zed.

"It's just a metal box," replied Lenny, as he climbed out of the hole holding a square rusty box, partly covered in mud.

"Let's not open it here in case we are seen," said George.

"We can open it in my home," said Zed.

"Yes, I think that would be a good idea," replied Lenny.

They all made their way into Zed's house, filled with excitement and expectation of the possible prospect of finding treasure. They sat quietly for a few minutes around a small table staring at the box.

"Anyone for tea?" said Zed, finally breaking the silence.

Eric was the only one to reply as the others were far too occupied with the box. You would have thought that they would jump to open the box; instead, it was the complete opposite. The thought of finding treasure had made them nervous. Zed brought four cups of tea and a plateful of cakes, for which Eric was obliged.

"I think we should clean it first," said Lenny.

Zed brought in a bowl of hot water and a cloth and Lenny got to work cleaning the box and, as the mud slowly washed off, it began to reveal a small padlock on the side and on the top a plate with an inscription, which read, "Ernest the Elephant."

"Here, Eric, didn't you once tell me you had a great-grandfather called Ernest?" said George.

"Now that you mention it, I did," replied Eric.

"You sure?" said Lenny, who was hoping to claim it for himself.

"One hundred percent sure, and I believe this could be my great-grandfather's treasure that my grandfather told me about," replied Eric as Lenny, Zed and George's faces lit up at the thought of possible treasure in the box.

"Tell us more, Eric" replied Zed, capturing not just his, but Lenny and George's attention.

"When I was young, my grandfather told me that my great-grandfather Ernest buried some treasure worth thousands, and that he died before telling anyone where he buried it; there's not really much more to say," said Eric.

"Hey, that's why you've been digging those holes in your sleep. You must have been dreaming about it and somehow, in your subconscious, you went looking for the treasure," said George.

"We've waited far too long. Zed, bring something to open the box," demanded Lenny.

Zed obeyed; he quickly went and found a hammer and gave it to Lenny, who grabbed it and with one hit broke open the padlock. Eric, George and Zed moved closer as Lenny slowly lifted the squeaky lid open to reveal its contents. Inside was not the treasure that was eagerly anticipated, but a rolled-up parchment, which Lenny did not hesitate to unroll.

"What is it?" asked George.

"It looks like a map," replied Zed.

"I think it could be a map leading to where Ernest buried his treasure," said Lenny.

"You mean a treasure map?" said Eric.

"Yes," replied Lenny.

"Wow, a treasure map, how exciting!" said George.

"According to the X, it's on that island," said Lenny.

"Eric, you're a rich elephant!" said George, patting Eric on the back.

"Why Eric? I found it!" said Lenny, rolling up the map in case it was taken from him.

"It should belong to Eric, since it was his great grandfather's," said George, in Eric's defence.

"There's no proof of that," said Lenny.

"Actually, it should belong to me, since it was in my garden," interrupted Zed.

"No, I found it!" argued Lenny.

"No, it should belong to Eric!" yelled George.

"It was found on my property!" yelled Zed.

"Quiet!" yelled Eric, silencing them all. "Why don't we all go together to find it?"

Everyone eventually agreed and swore to keep their discovery a secret. Eric was allowed to look after the map as they left Zed's house, agreeing to meet in the morning to discuss what they were going to do next.

Over the next few days, no more holes appeared; things settled down around the jungle. The mysterious holes remained a mystery to everyone and were eventually forgotten about, except for by Lenny, Zed, Eric and George who had made plans to travel to the island to find Ernest the Elephant's treasure. They had paid Barry the Beaver to make them a boat and were extremely pleased to hear that it would be ready the next day.

Lenny left his house the next morning in high spirits as he met with George and Eric, who had packed a rucksack each, mainly full of food. They arrived at Barry's boat yard to see Zed had already made himself at home, sitting on deck with his sailor's hat; he did look like he had been sailing all his life. Actually, the frightening thing was that not one of them knew how to sail.

Zed nominated himself to sail the boat, insisting that he should, since he was the one with the sailor's hat. The others didn't object, and were actually relieved that they did not have to do it. With great enthusiasm, Zed took the helm and – after several attempts to manoeuvre out of the boat yard – they were eventually heading out into the open sea. With the wind blowing in their sails and an hour of arguments figuring out how to navigate and read the map, they were finally sailing on the right course.

The sun shone brightly over the peaceful, calm ocean as Eric, George and Lenny sat on deck basking in the sun, while Zed remained behind the wheel, making sure they were heading in the right direction.

"This is the life, hey, Georgie-boy?" said Eric, munching on a corn on the cob.

"It sure is," replied George, feasting on a bunch of grapes.

"I can see now why you guys do this a lot," said Lenny, resting his paws behind his head as he leaned back in his chair.

"I don't know why we haven't thought of this before," said Eric, washing down a mouthful of grapes with some of his homemade tropical juice.

"Better late than never, I say," replied George.

"I could certainly do this more often," said Eric.

"Yeah, me too; the cool sea breeze, the beautiful blue ocean, it beats our lawn, hands down!" replied George.

"Once we find the treasure, we could be doing this for the rest of our lives..." laughed Eric.

"I couldn't agree more," said George, even though doing nothing is what they did anyway, whether at sea or on dry land.

"Me too," added Lenny, raising his cocktail glass in agreement.

For the rest of the day, George, Eric and Lenny did more or less nothing but laze around on deck, eating and drinking to their heart's content. It may have looked like the others were taking advantage of Zed but, in fact, he loved every minute of the experience and, as the day went on, he had gotten quite good at sailing.

While the sunbathing trio were enjoying the fantastic view of the sun setting, Zed decided to continue the journey in the morning, and lowered the anchor and sail. The boat slowly came to a stop and Zed was able to take a well-deserved rest.

"I'm hungry, guys; what's on the menu?" said Zed as he joined the rest on deck.

"Yeah, I could do with a bit to eat," replied Lenny rubbing his stomach.

"Great; where's the food?" asked Zed.

"We put it all in Eric's rucksack," said George.

"Is this all the food we have?" asked Zed, worriedly, when he opened the rucksack and looked inside.

"Yeah, how much more do you want?" replied George, bemused.

"Well, a lot more than what's in here," said Zed, passing it over for George to look inside.

"What? Where's it all gone? There was a load in here!" replied a surprised George.

"You guys have eaten it all and you didn't think of saving anything for me?" said Zed furiously.

"Don't look at me; I've hardly eaten anything," said

Lenny honestly.

"Me neither," said George.

"Then who has?" said Zed.

They all turned and looked at Eric, who was holding an apple and a stick of bread with his mouth, covered in food of all kinds.

"Eric!" shouted Zed, Lenny and George at once.

"I'm sorry; I didn't realise how much I'd eaten," replied Eric apologetically.

"That's typical, Eric – you always think about yourself!" yelled Lenny.

"Yeah, Lenny's right, Eric; you're so selfish!" replied Zed angrily.

"I'm really disappointed in you, Eric," said George "I mean, you never thought of saving me anything."

"I'm sorry, guys, I didn't realise," replied Eric softly.

"Didn't realise? I've got a good mind to throw you to the sharks!" shouted Lenny.

"Maybe we should..." added Zed.

"No, guys, let's be reasonable, we don't want to do something we'll regret..." said George.

"Reasonable? "We don't have enough food to last us the rest of the journey!" exclaimed Lenny.

"Then what do you suggest we do?" said George.

"Feed him to the sharks, for a start," replied Lenny.

"Come on, Lenny, let's be serious; what's done is done, we can't change things now. I'm just as annoyed with Eric as you are but we now have to be practical," said George.

"How far have we got left to go?" Lenny asked Zed.

"Let's go and check the map," replied Zed.

Zed took out the map and opened it out for the others to see as they gathered around him.

"Well, according to the map, we are here," said Zed, pointing to a spot of the ocean on the map. "The island is here and I estimate we could be there in about three days' time..."

"We don't even have enough food for one day, let alone three!" stressed Lenny. "Thanks to you, Eric, we're going to starve!"

"I can't apologise enough, Lenny..." said Eric, glumly.

"Well, I don't accept your apology, Eric, if you'd like to know!" replied Lenny.

"Stop arguing, guys, I think I've got an idea!" said Zed.

Again they all gathered around the map as Zed began to explain his idea.

"After looking at the map, we have two choices. The first choice is that we could strictly ration the food and head straight for the island, or the second choice is to head for this other island to gather more food, which

I have estimated would take us a day and half to get to. Although taking the second option would, in fact, delay us in reaching our destination."

"I'm in no hurry; we should go and get more food," said Lenny.

"I think we should head straight there," said George.

"You're joking! I'm not planning to eat crumbs when we could arrive a few days later well-fed!" said Lenny.

"I tell you what, why don't we put it to a vote? The majority wins," said Zed. "All those in favour of the first option, say 'yes'."

"Yes," said George by himself.

"Second option it is, then," said Lenny gladly.

"That's it, then; in the morning, we're heading for that island!" replied Zed.

Zed was up early the next morning setting sail on their new course. The others were still fast asleep, which was the best thing for them, as while they slept they did not feel hungry. Last night they just had a morsel to eat between them. Well, between Lenny, Zed and George, that is. Eric was excluded from eating until the morning.

After a few hours later, and after a very small breakfast (this time Eric was included), the trio – Lenny, George and Eric – were, once again, on deck sunbathing, with Zed happily at the helm. Everyone had made their peace with Eric, on the condition that he had the smallest ration of food. Eric reluctantly agreed, so as to end the cold silence.

They arrived at the island at mid-afternoon the next day. With great excitement, they ran straight for the delicious ripe fruit as soon as Zed brought the boat to a stop along the shore. They all spent the rest of the afternoon eating until their stomachs could fit no more; even Eric reached his limit.

"We'd better spend the night here," suggested Zed, "and in the morning, we could gather enough food to last us until we get to the island."

The others agreed and, after finding a nice sheltered area, they all settled down for the night. The next morning they woke up early after a peaceful night's sleep and, after collecting plenty of food, they set sail in search of Eric's great-grandfather's treasure.

"According to the map, we should reach the island in about four days, so let's not get carried away with the food," said Zed.

"You hear that, Eric? We're not to get carried away, okay?" replied Lenny sarcastically.

Eric said nothing and chose to ignore Lenny. He knew he had done wrong, but felt he could not help himself as he had the biggest appetite, being an elephant. The others were not so sympathetic and prevented Eric from having any access to the food. Eric had no choice, other than to agree to their terms, and focused his mind on the thought of finding his great-grandfather's treasure.

The rest of the day was spent lounging around on deck as Zed did his usual thing of sailing the boat. It was George who noticed that the sky had slowly become cloudy and, after an hour, it was filled with black clouds.

"That doesn't look good..." said George, looking up at the sky.

"It looks like a storm's brewing," replied Zed.

"That's not a good thing, is it?" asked a quite concerned Lenny.

"It depends on how big the storm is," answered Zed.

"Looking at those clouds, we could be in for quite a storm," said George, not making things any better.

"Is there any way we could avoid it?" asked Lenny.

"I'm afraid I don't think we can avoid it now," replied Zed. "It looks like we're going to hit the storm whichever way we go..."

"Let's hope it's not going to be a big one," said Lenny.

"Yeah; hope is all we can do right now," replied Zed trying to be optimistic.

It did not take long for it to rain spits and spats at first, followed by a light shower, before the clouds gave way to a very heavy downpour. Lenny and George quickly lowered the sail as the wind became stronger. It blew the boat violently, tossing around everyone inside.

"We're going to die!" yelled Eric, clinging to the boat

for his life. "I'm too young to die!"

"Calm down, Eric, this is no time to get hysterical" replied Zed, who gripped the helm firmly, trying in vain to keep the boat on course.

The storm continued well into the night, with the torrential rain and violent winds refusing to ease off, and with wave after wave bombarding the boat, it was starting to show signs of damage. This began to worry the crew a great deal... especially when the mast broke off.

"If we don't get out of this storm quickly, there'll be nothing left of the boat!" exclaimed Lenny.

"We're going to die!" screamed Eric.

"Oh, shut it, Eric!" yelled Lenny, George and Zed together.

"We need to change course... and fast!" said George.

"Where do you suggest we go? If you haven't noticed, we're in a storm!" replied Zed sarcastically, hiding his fear.

"You're the one navigating!" yelled George.

"It's hard to steer the boat; the winds are too strong!" replied Zed.

"But you still can," said Lenny.

"What's your point?" asked Zed.

"My point is that, if we don't try and get out of this storm, we'll be building our homes at the bottom of the ocean!" replied Lenny.

"It won't be easy: the wind's too strong..." explained Zed.

"Where are we anyway?" asked George.

"We're...We're..." replied Zed.

"You've have no idea, do you?" said George worriedly.

"I'm not sure, we've been blown off course," replied Zed.

"Which means we could be anywhere," said Lenny.

"We're going to die!" said Eric, terrified, looking up at a huge wave that was about to fall upon the boat.

"Everyone hold on tight!" yelled Zed.

The wave proved too much for the fragile boat and it was smashed to pieces as it became submerged by the falling gigantic wave. The jungle animals' treasure hunt was over.

The sun shone brightly the next morning after a horrendous stormy night. Lenny woke up staring up at the cloudless blue sky and thought for a moment that last night's battle with the storm was a dream, until he turned his head, expecting to see George or Eric sunbathing next to him. Instead he found himself washed up on a beach. He sat up and looked around, hoping to see any of the others, but there was no sign of them. He stood up, deeply concerned for his three friends, and set off along the beach in search of them. He found George dazed, but in one piece, several yards along the beach.

"I'm so glad to see you!" said Lenny, overjoyed to see George alive.

"Where are we?" asked George.

"An island, I think," replied Lenny.

"Eric? Have you seen Eric?" asked George hysterically.

"No not a sign of either Eric or Zed," answered Lenny.

"We should look for them; maybe they're here too," said George.

"Sure, only if you can," said Lenny.

"Yeah I'm fine, let's go," replied George, standing up.

"Good – I'll go this way, you take that way, and meet back here when we finish or if we find the others," said Lenny marking a cross in the sand to represent the meeting point.

They both searched the beach until they could not go any further, but found no sign of Eric or Zed and, when they met back at the cross, their emotions could not be contained.

"He's gone, Lenny... my dearest friend," sobbed George looking at the ocean.

"They were good friends," cried Lenny also looking at the ocean.

"It won't be the same on the lawn without him," whimpered George.

"I feel bad that I treated Eric so badly," wailed Lenny.

"Me too," replied George.

"It's hard to believe we will never see them again," said Lenny.

"I know; it's so hard that I'm imagining I can see Zed floating out there in the sea," said George.

"I can see him too!" replied Lenny.

"You can?" asked George, puzzled.

"Yeah, I see him right there, floating on some sort of raft!" replied Lenny.

"How strange, I see the same thing," George said.

"You do?" replied Lenny confused.

"Yeah, what a coincidence!" said George.

"George, don't you see? That's no illusion, that's really Zed!" exclaimed Lenny.

"What?" replied George, bemused. "It's a ghost?""No, it's him, it's really him!" yelled Lenny, jumping for joy.

"My goodness, you're right!" replied George ecstatically.

While George and Lenny danced around, Zed – who was lying on a piece of the boat's deck –was paddling with his front legs towards the shore and, before long, he embraced his two friends, who were jubilant to see him.

"We thought you were a goner for sure," said Lenny.

"I was fortunate to find this piece of the boat's deck, so I climbed onto it. I don't remember anything else until I woke up and saw this island in the distance," explained Zed.

"It's so great to see you okay," replied Lenny.

"Where's Eric?" asked Zed.

"We don't know," answered Lenny.

"We were hoping you might know..." said George.

"I haven't seen him, not since the storm," said Zed dolefully.

It did not go down too well with George as he walked off very distraught.

"He's taking it quite bad," said Lenny.

"I'm not surprised, they've been friends for a very long time," replied Zed.

The trio sat looking towards the sea for over an hour. The weather took a familiar look about it as the blue sky soon became filled with black clouds.

"It looks like there's going to be a storm again," said Zed.

"You're right – and it looks like a big one," replied Lenny.

"I think we'd better build a shelter for ourselves," said Zed.

Lenny and George agreed, and they were soon off collecting materials. They all settled to building their own shelters but George, who was not in the mood, opted for some tall grass he found nearby. Lenny was a bit more adventurous and decided on wood, using branches, and Zed, who was even more ambitious, built his shelter with stones and mud.

Lenny and George had already completed their temporary homes by the time Zed had finished his. It was nightfall when the storm arrived. The rain fell heavily and the wind blew hard as they slept peacefully, but it was all about to change. As the wind huffed and puffed, George's home was the first to be blown away. He ran and took shelter with Lenny, but a little while later the wind blow his stick house away too. They then had no option but to take shelter with Zed; fortunately for them, the stone shelter remained standing.

The next morning the sun took centre stage against the blue sky as Zed, Lenny and George emerged from the stone shelter feeling stiff, but despite the cramped conditions, they had all slept peacefully.

"That was quite a storm last night," said Zed, looking at the debris scattered all over the beach.

"It sure was," replied Lenny.

"Thanks for having us," said George.

"Don't mention it; what was I to do, leave you guys out here all night?" replied Zed.

"Who's for breakfast?" asked Lenny.

"Yeah, what's on the menu?" replied Zed.

"Whatever the island has for us," said Lenny, pointing to the trees.

"Great, I'm starving," replied George.

They all made their way into the jungle to look for what they could find to eat. As they approached the trees, they heard something from inside the jungle which sounded like it was coming towards them.

"What could it be?" asked George.

"We'd better stand back, it could be wild natives" replied Zed.

"Well, I'm ready for them," said Lenny, holding a huge stick he had found amongst the debris on the beach.

The footsteps grew louder and louder and soon they could see movement from the trees.

"My goodness... whatever it is, it's very big!" exclaimed George.

"I'd better get a bigger stick!" said Lenny.

"I don't think there's time, it's here," said Zed, clinging tightly to George.

Out from the trees stepped an animal... but, due to the pineapples, coconuts, bananas, melons, mangoes and passion fruit it was holding, they could not see what it was.

"Don't take a step further or I'll knock you straight to the moon!" yelled Lenny, lifting the stick above his head, preparing to take a swing.

This startled the newcomer, causing him to throw all the fruit into the air and, as gravity goes, it shortly fell down upon Zed, George and Lenny. After a few seconds recovering from the shock of being hit by the falling fruit, right in front of them, as clear as glass, stood Eric, wearing the biggest grin you would ever see.

"Eric!" yelled George ecstatically.

"Georgie-boy!" replied Eric, just as joyful.

After celebrating their reunion they all sat down together on the beach, ate the delicious fruit that Eric had picked, and listened to his story. He explained that, yesterday, he had found himself on the beach on the other side of the island and, driven by hunger, he had made his way into the jungle, collecting fruit on the way.

"Where did you spend the night?" asked George biting into a melon.

"Oh, I was fortunate to find a cave to escape that terrible storm," replied Eric.

"How did you know to come here?" asked Zed.

"I didn't; I just continued to pick fruit and I ended up here," replied Eric before shoving two bananas into his mouth.

"Well, I'm so glad to see you, I thought I was never

going to see you again!" said George.

"Happy to be here!" replied Eric.

After eating their fill, they all lay on the beach with full stomachs, content and happy that everyone was alive, until Lenny remembered the treasure.

"The map, the map, who's got the map?" yelled Lenny.

"Oh yeah, we forgot about that," said George. "Zed, I believe you had it last?"

"Zed, please tell me you have the map," asked Lenny desperately.

"I'm sorry; I must have left it on the boat," replied Zed apologetically.

"What? How can you be so stupid?" roared Lenny, angrily jumping onto Zed and grabbing his throat with both his paws.

"Help!" screamed Zed as Lenny tightened his grip and began to choke him.

Eric and George came to the rescue as they pulled Lenny off Zed, who frantically tried to get his breath back.

"You crazy lion, you almost killed me!" yelled Zed.

"Crazy? I'll show you I'm crazy!" yelled Lenny, fighting to free himself from Eric and George's clutches.

"Lenny, that's enough!" yelled George, forcing Lenny to the ground before sitting on him.

"Calm down, Lenny, it's not Zed's fault," said Eric trying to extinguish his anger.

"Yeah, you're right, Eric, it's not Zed's fault, it's yours!" replied Lenny, pouncing on Eric.

"Help!" shrieked Eric as Lenny seized his throat.

"If it was not for your greed, we would not have had to change course, and we would not have been in that storm!" roared Lenny.

"Come on, Lenny, this won't change anything!" pleaded George.

"But it will make me feel better!" said Lenny angrily.

George and Zed eventually managed to pull Lenny off and after a few minutes he c

almed down before apologising to both Zed and Eric.

No-one spoke for a while, as they were all coming to terms with the loss of the map, and the thought of never finding Eric's great-grandfather's treasure. Zed was first to break the silence.

"Eric, did you see anyone else on this island?" he asked.

"No, sorry," replied Eric. "I was too busy picking fruit to check."

"Hah, typical," said Lenny under his breath, quickly receiving a stern look from both George and Zed.

"I think we should figure out a way off this island," said Zed.

"What are you planning to do – sail the island home?" said Lenny sarcastically.

"If you're not going to say anything constructive I'd rather you said nothing," replied Zed firmly.

"Face it, Zed: how on earth are we going to leave this island?" said Lenny.

"Be positive, Lenny; I'm sure there's loads of ways off this island," replied Zed.

"Name one!" said Lenny.

"Err... err... we could make a boat, we've got loads of trees," replied Zed quickly.

"Yeah, great idea... but two things. One: none of us can build a boat, and two: we don't have any tools, and especially tools to cut down those trees," said Lenny, making his point.

"Point taken," replied Zed.

"That's it, then; we have no other option than to spend the rest of our lives here," said Lenny.

"Or we could find out where that smoke is coming from," said Eric, pointing towards the plume of smoke above the tree tops.

"There's someone else on the island!" shouted Zed with excitement.

"Well, what are we waiting for? Let's go!" said Lenny, already making his way into the jungle.

"Wait! We don't know if they're friendly!" yelled George.

"It's a risk I'm prepared to take!" yelled back Lenny.

"I'm going with Lenny," said Zed, heading into the jungle after him.

"Well, I'm staying here with Eric," George shouted back.

"Sorry, Georgie-boy, but I'm going with the others," said Eric as he, too, went into the jungle after Zed and Lenny.

"Well, I'm staying put," insisted George, but the thought of being alone soon changed his mind. "Wait for me!" he yelled, running after the others.

Hours later, and after a long walk through dense vegetation, they finally reached the source of the smoke and what they saw truly amazed them. In the middle of a small clearing was a wooden house. The smoke billowed out from a small fire that was burning vigorously in front of the house.

"I wonder what's for dinner?" said Eric.

"Hello? Anyone home?" called Lenny loudly.

"Shh! Don't you think it would be wise to wait and see first whether whoever is friendly?" whispered George.

"No, I'm hungry and I want to get off this island!" replied Lenny.

Just as Lenny was about to call again, out stepped the mystery inhabitant, holding a huge fish he planned to cook on the fire. To Lenny's surprise, standing gobsmacked in front of them stood a lion, who Lenny recognised immediately. "Lawrence!"

"Oh, my goodness; how did you find me?" replied Lawrence, dropping his fish and running back into his house."Wait! Lawrence, it's me Lenny, your cousin," replied Lenny.

"Somehow I don't think he was pleased to see us," said George.

"He can't still be mad about that time he came to visit," replied Lenny.

"It's obvious he's still sour about his trip to the Karoomba," said Zed.

"Lawrence, if this is about what happened when you came to visit, I'd like to apologise about what happened – it was a complete misunderstanding. No-one meant to harm you," said Lenny.

"You're liars, all of you. You're here to kill me!" replied Lawrence from the window.

"That's nonsense," said Lenny.

"Why are you here, then, if it's not to kill me?" replied Lawrence.

"We were shipwrecked here," said Lenny. "We only want to go home."

"You are telling the truth, right?" replied Lawrence stepping out of his house.

"Of course we are," said Lenny.

After some gentle persuasion, Lawrence felt safe enough to invite them inside his house. While the fish cooked outside with a pot of vegetable stew for Zed, Eric and George, Lenny explained to Lawrence everything that had happened since the time he had visited Karoomba, including about Eric's great-grandfather's buried treasure and how they ended up on the island. Lawrence eventually saw the funny side of what had happened to him in the Karoomba jungle and forgave them, which Lenny was much relieved about.

"I could do with a break from this place," said Lawrence while he served everyone food. "I've been on my own for a long time. You guys coming here has made me realise that I miss having someone to talk to."

"I'm surprised you haven't gone mad," said Lenny.

"Well, I've decided. Before I do go crazy, how about I take you guys home tomorrow morning?" replied Lawrence.

"Yes, we'd love you to!" answered Lenny on everyone's behalf. "How?"

"With my boat, of course!" replied Lawrence.

They spent the rest of the day (and most of the night) around the fire telling wild stories and Lenny was surprised to learn about Lawrence and a certain bunch of beans he used as payment to cross a bridge, which was guarded by a half-crazed goat. Lenny chose not to mention anything about his encounter with the beans, and gestured with his eyes to the others not to say anything either, so that he could be spared embarrassment.

Lawrence was up at the crack of dawn to prepare his boat for the long journey to the Karoomba jungle while the others were still fast asleep. When they finally woke, Lawrence had just finished collecting food for the trip. After breakfast, they all boarded the boat, and after several minutes the island was just a mere speck on the horizon.

Four days later they reached home and things returned to normal. Lenny, Zed, George and Eric never forgot their adventure. In fact, despite all their disagreements and arguments, their friendship had become stronger. Eric and George wasted no time setting up their deckchairs and finding their spot on the lawn. Lawrence, after spending a month with Lenny, returned back to his island and promised to return again sometime in the near future. As for Eric's great-grandfather's treasure, it was never found.

The End

....

Eric learnt that his selfishness had put his friends in danger, and that there is nothing gained by being selfish. Lenny also learnt about how forgiveness ends bitterness. He was thankful that his cousin Lawrence forgave them, otherwise they would have been stuck on the island.

The Bible warns us that selfish behaviour brings all kinds of problems, and that it is not God's kind of wisdom and it has no place in his kingdom. Going back to the story, Eric's selfishness shows the problems it caused to all his friends. Thinking of others, instead of just ourselves, is what we should do and is the sort of behaviour that pleases God.

God always forgives us, so he expects us to always forgive everyone who wrongs us, even though we may find it hard to do, and most of the time it restores relationships, just like it did with Lawrence and Lenny. Forgiveness is not only an act of love, but it heals us from angry emotions that we can carry around with us. So, if you are feeling bitter with someone or a circumstance, don't dwell on it for long, otherwise it will the root of bitterness will grow deeper and, not only will it steal your joy, but may become harder to overcome. Learn to settle differences quickly, and ask God to help you, and to also heal you.

James 3:15-16, Luke 6:37, 17:4, Mark 11:25

KING LIONEL

I'm always reminded of the importance of humility when I tell this tale of when the jungle was visited by someone very special, and how this special person touched the lives of many.

It was cup fever in the Karoomba, as animals from all over the jungle flocked into the Karoomba national football stadium to see the end-of-season cup final, between the league champions, Karoomba Lions, and the underdogs, the Grassland Jackals. This year, to add to the excitement of the prospect of a great game, His Royal Highness King Lionel the Lion was expected to attend. It would be the first time a monarch attended since Queen Linda the Lioness had watched the match between the Savannah Cheetahs and the Rebel Rhinos, over twenty years ago.

Lifelong Lions fans Lenny, Leo, Larry, Luther and Lester, filled with excitement, made their way towards the stadium, singing loudly to themselves. Along the way they met George, who was also a fan, and Eric, who had no interest in football at all, and was only going because

George had bought him a ticket.

"It's going to be a great game, don't you think?" Lenny asked George jubilantly.

"It sure will be," replied George. "You agree, Eric?"

"Yeah, wonderful," said Eric, acting interested.

"What's up with him?" asked Lenny, puzzled by Eric's lack of enthusiasm.

"Oh, ignore him, Lenny; he doesn't appreciate the beautiful game" replied George.

"Beautiful? What's so beautiful about a bunch of animals running around kicking a ball?" said Eric.

"Don't worry, George, that's exactly what my wife says every time I watch football," replied Larry.

"I suppose you either like it or you don't," said George. "Well, you never know; he might change his mind once it starts..."

"I doubt it," replied Eric.

The chants grew louder as they approached the stadium and, when they entered, the atmosphere was breathtaking. Hundreds of animals had already taken their seats and, when King Lionel arrived and sat in the royal box, everyone stood up and gave him a welcome round of applause.

"Are you comfortable in your seat, Your Highness?" asked Edmond the Elk, the King's Royal Affairs Adviser.

"Yes, Edmond, I am fine," replied King Lionel.

"Would you like a cushion, Your Highness?" said Edmond.

"No, I'm comfortable as I am," replied the King.

"A drink; would you like a drink?" asked Edmond.

"No, I am fine," replied the King.

"Something to eat, maybe?" asked Edmond.

"Edmond, I'm fine; I do not want a cushion, I do not want a drink, I do not want anything to eat and my seat is fine," replied King Lionel sternly. "Now be quiet and watch the pre-match entertainment, it is about to start!"

"Yes, Your Highness," replied Edmond softly.

The stadium came alive when the entertainment began warming up the spectators for the main event.

"It looks like a full house today," said Lenny.

"Yeah, I'm getting excited already!" replied George.

"I can't ever think why," said Eric, not sharing George's emotions.

"You wait, you'll change your mind once the game's finished," replied George.

"I won't hold my breath," said Eric.

After the pre-match entertainment, which still left Eric unexcited, the two commentators, holding a megaphone, each took to their seats and began to announce the start of the match.

"Well, here it is Olsen, the twenty-sixth Karoomba cup final!" said Keith the Kangaroo through his megaphone.

"Yes, and what a mouth-watering final we're going to get. Two great technical passing teams and neither are shy of scoring goals!" replied Olsen the Orang-utan.

"Yes, you're right, both teams between them have scored a staggering twenty-two goals so far in this cup competition, and let's not forget how tight their defence has been as well!" said Keith passionately.

"Let's talk about the Karoomba Lions, the new league champions; they've been impressive this season, haven't they Keith?"

"Impressive isn't the word, they've been awesome! They have played great football throughout the season, especially Leon – their centre-forward – who started the season slowly, but eventually burst into form with twenty-seven league goals this season!" said Keith.

"Yes, he certainly is the one to watch today. So tell me, Keith; if the Lions are to win this match and do an historic league and cup double, which of the players is going to stand out and possibly win it for the Lions?" said Olsen. "Well, there are number of players in the Lions' team that, on the day, could be outstanding. But if the Lions are to win, I think centre-forward Leon and midfielder Luke have to perform to their world-class abilities!" replied Keith.

"Do you think that, without the injured Lance, they may struggle in defence?" asked Olsen.

"Missing a world-class player like Lance is a huge loss, but the Lions do have quality in their squad; I'm sure it's going to be a big test for Liam, who has been called in to replace Lance, but he'll be alright," said Keith.

"What about the Jackals? What a great achievement for them to reach their first final!" said Olsen.

"Yeah, this is what I love about this cup; the fact that teams like the Grassland Jackals can reach a domestic final is great, isn't it?" replied Keith.

"That's the romance of this cup competition! If you look at the Jackals' record this season, it's been poor, finishing fifteenth four points above the relegation zone!" said Olsen.

"Everyone had high expectations for the Jackals to finish in the top six; a win here today could make up for such a poor season!" said Keith.

"So tell me, Keith; what can the Jackals do to beat the Lions and win this cup?" asked Olsen.

"Well, there's no doubt that it's going to be a tough game for them, especially with the Lions on such form; one defeat in the last eighteen is quite impressive. But you know, the thing with this cup competition is that form goes out the window, and if the Jackals are to win, they are going to have to stop the Lions' midfield from playing their passing game and keep Leon tightly marked," said Keith.

"Who do you think could do that?" asked Olsen.

"That's a tough question, Olsen; who can do that? I think the two centre-halves, Jake and Jamie, have to be on top of their game. The midfield duo of Jasper and Joel has to keep Luke and Leroy quiet, and their top goal-scorer Jermaine has to perform today," said Keith.

"It does look like a tough task for the Jackals, but who knows?" replied Olsen.

"Exactly, Olsen; it would be amazing if they could pull it off today!" said Keith excitedly.

"Wouldn't it just?" replied Olsen.

Kick-off was fast approaching and, as the two teams emerged from the tunnel into the stadium, there was an eruption of cheers from both sets of fans. The Karoomba Lions were led out by their coach, Lex the Lion, and walking alongside the Lions were the Grassland Jackals following their coach, Jacob the Jackal. Both teams lined up horizontally, facing the royal box, while the Bobcat Babes sang the Karoomba national anthem. When they stopped singing, the King and the chairman of the KFA (Karoomba Football Association) came down from the royal box to meet the players. When this was done, it was back to the commentators to announce both teams.

"This is it; kick-off's minutes away, so here's Keith with the team line-up!" said Olsen.

"Thank you, Olsen; I'll begin with the Karoomba Lions playing a four-five-one formation with Lucas in goal; Lee, Liam, Louie, and Lloyd in defence; Leroy, Leslie, Luke, Lenard, Lawrence; and Leon, the lone striker, up front who will have Luke playing just behind him. The Grassland Jackals, playing four-four-two, have Jimmy in goal; Jansen, Jake, Jamie and Jamal in defence; Jeffery, Jasper, Joel and Jackson in midfield; and Jermaine and Jack up front," Keith said.

"Well, it looks like kick-off is seconds away, Keith... and it's the Jackals who have won the toss and have decided to kick off first..." said Olsen.

"So it's the Jackals to kick off, wearing their familiar yellow shirts and green shorts, and the Lions defending the goal to our left wearing their all-red strip," said Keith.

"The referee blows his whistle.... and we're off, the twenty-sixth cup final is underway!" yelled Olsen with excitement.

The crowd roared jubilantly as the game got underway and continued to sing and chant throughout the first half of the match. With some entertaining end-to-end football with both teams hitting the crossbar, the Karoomba Lions ended the half one goal up, with the goal scored by Leon after twenty-nine minutes.

The first fifteen minutes of the second half failed to live up to the expectations and excitement of the first, but when Jermaine equalised for the Jackals on sixty-three minutes, it sent the Jackal spectators wild and, soon after that, the game improved. But the Jackals' revival was short lived as the Lions soon turned up a gear and began to dominate the match and, after continuous pressure, at seventy-two minutes the team's captain, Lloyd, headed in their second goal from a corner. From that point on, two-one down, it was all uphill for the Jackals. There was some hope when Luke missed a penalty, but in the eighty-eighth minute, Luke sealed it for the Lions with a superb curling free kick that left Jimmy no chance of saving.

The final whistle blew and it was all over for the Jackals, going down three goals to one, despite playing exceptionally well. After the Lions lifted the cup (making history by being the first team to complete the league and cup double), they did a lap of honour in front of their fans.

"That was a great game," said Lenny as he, George and Eric left the stadium.

"One of the best I've seen," replied George.

"What about you, Eric; did you enjoy it too?" asked Lenny.

"Yeah, it was great," replied Eric.

"What do you mean? You slept through the whole match!" said George.

"Exactly! That was what was so great!" replied Eric.

While the highly-jubilant Lion fans and not-so-much Jackal fans slowly left the stadium, King Lionel remained seated.

"Is everything alright, Your Highness?" asked Edmond.

"Yes, I have really enjoyed myself. It was quite entertaining," replied King Lionel.

"But you look like you haven't," said Edmond.

"I did... but I believe I would have had more fun if I sat amongst the spectators," replied King Lionel.

"What do you mean?" asked Edmond, puzzled.

"Well, I noticed that everyone was having so much fun that I really wanted to join them," replied the king.

"That would be insane, Your Highness!" exclaimed Edmond.

"And why would it?" replied the king sternly.

"Well, you can't possibly mix with common animals, Your Highness, you're royalty," said Edmond.

"That's exactly my point, Edmond," replied King Lionel.

"I don't understand, Your Highness," said Edmond, completely baffled by the king's behaviour.

"I've been thinking, Edmond. All my life I've had everything I wanted, although I grew up with many restrictions, and the first time I do something different – like watching this cup final – I'm still restricted," explained King Lionel.

"We can always come again, Your Highness," said Edmond.

"You still don't understand, Edmond," replied the king.

"I don't?" replied Edmond, confused.

"I've decided that, as of next week and until my next birthday, I'm going to live like a normal animal, right here in the jungle," said King Lionel.

"Your Highness, you don't know the first thing about living amongst these commoners!" replied Edmond.

"You're right; that's why you're coming with me!" said the king.

"What! Your Highness, I couldn't possibly do this," protested Edmond.

"Well, I've just have to find myself another Royal Affairs Advisor..." said King Lionel, knowing it would change Edmond's mind.

"Did I say I wasn't coming? You misunderstood, Your Highness, what I really meant was that I couldn't possibly do this until I've found us a really nice place to stay," replied Edmond, changing his mind quickly.

"Great! I'll leave you to sort it all out!" said the king as they left the stadium.

"You weren't really going to find another advisor?" asked Edmond.

"Edmond! Edmond, would I do such a thing?" replied King Lionel.

"No, Your Highness; of course you wouldn't!" said Edmond, unenthusiastically but relieved.

The next day the jungle was unusually quiet, as most of it was deserted. The animals had all gathered outside the

Mayor's house to see the Karoomba Lions parade their two cups. Lenny, Leo, Larry, Luther and Lester were all there, as well as George, surprisingly without Eric, who said he rather watch paint dry than watch a bunch of lions getting excited over a piece of metal, stayed at home.

The crowd were waiting patiently beneath the Mayor's balcony for the team to emerge and when Toby the Tiger, the Mayor of Karoomba jungle appeared, the mass of Lions fans cheered loudly.

"Can I have your attention, please?" called Toby, and it went silent almost immediately.

"I'd like you, please, to all welcome the new league and cup double winning team: the Karoomba Lions!"

The crowd went hysterical as each player stepped out onto the balcony, with the Captain Lloyd holding the league cup and Luke and Leon together holding the Karoomba cup, and as they lifted them aloft, the crowd went wild and began to chant "Champions!" over and over again. The celebrations soon came to an end as the jungle animals left for home while some headed for Leo's fruit juice parlour. While everyone was leaving merrily, no-one noticed the two strangers who were also there, celebrating with them.

★

A week had passed; the excitement of the cup final had finally come to an end, and things around the jungle eventually returned back to normal, until the posters appeared. Around the jungle, the animals began to notice on some of the trees advertisements for odd-job services. This is what it said:Great news for all jungle dwellers!

If there is a job that's too hard for you

or a job you keep putting off

Then don't worry: Len's at hand to do the jobs you can't

or the jobs you hate!

Over the next few days, Len and his handy assistant will be passing by to fulfil all your needs.

Our services are all FREE of charge!

It soon became the talk of the jungle as the inhabitants waited anxiously for the mysterious Len to show, but they were – at the same time – excited at the prospect of someone who was willing to do all their distasteful jobs, especially all for free. The waiting was short-lived when a scruffy-looking lion wearing overalls, and a likewise elk, walked into Leo's fruit juice parlour.

"Your Highness, what are we doing here?" whispered Edmond, looking around at a mob of animals who were staring curiously at them the moment they walked in.

"Looking for a juice, of course" replied King Lionel.

"I know that, Your Highness, but it's full of ruffians," said Edmond, worriedly. "That rhino over there is looking at me in a very intimidating way."

"Don't be absurd, Edmond, and get in the drinks!" ordered the king.

"Yes, Your Highness, I'm onto it," replied Edmond. "What would you like?"

"Orange juice, please," answered King Lionel politely.

Edmond walked bravely over to Leo, although he kept one eye on the intimidating rhino.

"Good afternoon; what could I get you?" asked Leo, politely.

"Two orange juices please, sir," replied the elk.

"Forgive me for asking, but are you the Len that everyone's talking about?" asked Leo, passing over two glasses.

"Len?" replied Edmond, puzzled.

"Yeah, the one who's going to do all the odd jobs for free," said Leo.

"Oh yes, that would be him over there; I'm just his assistant," answered Edmond honestly.

"Great! Do you think he could give my parlour a paint job?" asked Leo.

"I shouldn't think it would be a problem," replied Edmond. "When can we book you in?"

"Tomorrow would be fine," answered Leo.

Edmond returned to King Lionel and explained everything to him about painting Leo's parlour, and discovered that the king had also booked in some jobs as well.

"It looks like we're in for a busy week," replied Edmond dolefully.

"We're going to have so much fun, Edmond – I wish we had done this sooner!" said the King joyfully.

"I can't wait," replied Edmond solemnly.

Three days later, back at their rented apartment sitting motionless in two armchairs with a cup of hot tea each and a plate with one half-eaten scone, King Lionel and Edmond were already feeling the strain. With Leo's parlour completely repainted, three mended fences, six gutters cleared and cleaned, and eight shelves assembled and fitted, they both wondered how they would last a week, let alone another two-and-a-half weeks until the king's birthday.

"Your Highness, I don't know if I can keep going at this rate," said Edmond. "I can't feel my feet and this cup feels like it weighs a ton..." he added.

"Oh, stop complaining, Edmond, aren't you having any fun?" replied the king, unsympathetically.

"I think, Your Highness, we have a different perspective on what you mean by fun," said Edmond."Oh, come on, Edmond; aren't you fascinated by how these animals live?" asked King Lionel.

"Not in the slightest," replied Edmond honestly.

"Well, you'd better, because tomorrow – after we complete all our jobs – Barbra has kindly invited us both to join her and her friends for dinner, and I have gladly accepted," said the king.

"Great, an evening with a bunch of baboons, how wonderful..." replied Edmond dolefully.

"We'd better get some sleep, we've got an early start tomorrow: we're painting Olivia the Ostrich's house," the king said.

Edmond did not reply; instead, he groaned as he made his way slowly and painfully to his bedroom.

It took King Lionel and Edmond most of the day to finish painting Olivia's house, the reason being that Erica the Emu also popped over and, between the two of them, Olivia and Erica had bombarded the King and Edmond with so much idle chatter that it took them forever to complete the painting – leaving them both exhausted, not only physically, but mentally as well.

"I've never heard so much chatter coming out of two birds' beaks in all my life," moaned Edmond as they left Olivia's house to go to their next job.

"It was a bit hard on the ears, I must admit," replied the king. "Still, they mean no harm."

They arrived at Barbra the Baboon's house by early evening, after they had decided to finish early, to wash and dress. Barbra assured them that the her guests had already arrived and, when they entered the dining room, sitting along a long table sat four baboons who seemed very happy to see them.

"Everyone, this is Len and his assistant," said Barbra

joyfully.

"Good evening, everyone," said King Lionel politely.

"Oh, good evening," replied all four baboons at the same time.

"Let me introduce you to my friends," said Barbra. "Sitting over there on the right is Beryl; sitting next to her is Beatrice; then Brenda, and finally Benjamin."

"Does your assistant have a name?" asked Brenda.

"His name is Ernest," replied King Lionel, answering for Edmond.

"Lost his tongue, has he?" said Brenda impolitely.

"Brenda, please be nice to our guests," said Barbra sternly. "I do apologise, Ernest."

"Your Highness, what have you dragged me into?" whispered Edmond.

"Just make an effort," replied King Lionel quietly.

"I will, but I'm only doing this for you!" whispered Edmond.

After a slow start, the evening soon began to liven up, as Barbra brought in course after course of very delicious food. Edmond managed to shrug off his moodiness and joined in with the conversations and, as the evening went on, he was really starting to enjoy the company of baboons. Benjamin, who hardly spoke throughout the evening, made the king and Edmond quite uncomfortable by the way he stared constantly at them. When Barbra brought in her huge triple-chocolate gâteau for dessert, it sent excitement around the table at the sight of the oozing chocolate as it dripped down the sides.

"I knew I recognised you!" yelled Benjamin, suddenly startling everybody, including Barbra, who almost dropped the gâteau.

"I beg your pardon?" replied Barbra, placing the dessert safely onto the table.

"I've been sitting here all this time wondering where I've seen him before, and I've suddenly realised who he is," explained Benjamin, referring to King Lionel. "He's an imposter!"

"Benjamin, you'd better have a good explanation for your rudeness," replied Barbra.

"He's not who he says he is!" said Benjamin "Don't you recognise him?"

"He properly looks like any other Lion..." replied Edmond, sensing that the king was becoming uncomfortable with Benjamin's accusations.

"Stop making excuses for him; you know very well who he is!" said Benjamin.

"Will anyone tell us what is going on?" interrupted Barbra loudly.

"I'll be glad to," replied Benjamin. "Our odd-job man Len is actually our very own King Lionel!" There was a short pause as ten pairs of eyes gazed straight at the king before Barbra, Beryl, Beatrice and Brenda all burst into fits of laughter. "You all can laugh as much as you want, I'm right and he knows it!" said Benjamin.

"Oh, come on, Benjamin; soon you're going to tell us that the Elk is the King's Royal Affairs Advisor!" laughed Brenda.

"That's right, he is; our very own Edmond." replied Benjamin.

"Oh, come on, Benjamin, that's absurd; do you think the king would go round doing all the hateful jobs, getting his royal hands dirty for nothing? You must have hit your head or something," said Barbra, defending King Lionel. "Len, I do apologise for my friend, but I think he must need to wear glasses or something; he may have a problem with his eyesight."

"My eyesight is perfectly well, thank you; it's all of yours that needs some attention!" replied Benjamin, in his own defence.

King Lionel saw that it was going to erupt into a full-scale argument and, ignoring Edmond's gestures, stood up to tell the truth.

"Everyone, Benjamin's telling the truth... I am the king!" said King Lionel, showing them his royal signet ring.

Again there was a short pause until Benjamin broke the silence.

"By jolly, it's true; I was just trying my luck!" he replied, just as surprised as the other baboons.

"My goodness – the king in my house! I would never have dreamed it!" said Barbra joyously.

"Your Highness, why pretend to be someone else? I don't understand," asked Brenda, as all of them, including Benjamin, fell to the floor in worship.King Lionel explained everything to them and, by the end of the week, all the jungle knew about Len and who he really was. Some believed, but sadly many did not; instead, they just mocked the king. By the end of the three-and-a-half weeks on the day of the King's Birthday, King Lionel organised a very big party to celebrate and all those who had believed him were invited.

The End

....

King Lionel amazed many animals by the way he gave up all his royal privileges to come and live amongst all the animals in the Karoomba jungle. All the animals who believed he was king will always remember him as the king who became a humble servant.

This is exactly what Jesus did for us. He gave up His divine privileges to live on Earth and to humbly serve human beings, returning them back to God, by showing them a better way to live. Just like in the story of King Lionel, many did not believe. It was the same with Jesus; many did not believe that He was the Messiah, God's only son. Instead they had Him crucified on a cross, which was God's plan – so that His son could die, instead of us. It does sound cruel, but Jesus died so that our sins can be forgiven, and that every believer is given eternal life. Jesus did not remain dead; He came back to life after three days to join His Father in Heaven, where He is preparing a new home for us and, when He is finished, He will return to Earth again, to get everyone who believes in Him to join Him in Heaven.

John 3:16, Matthew chapter 20:28, 20:18, Philippians 2:6. Read the four Gospels of Matthew, Mark, Luke and John.

OUT ON THE LAWN

It is only appropriate to finish off with a tale with Eric and George and, as all they ever do is laze around on their recliners, don't expect a very long one!Eric the Elephant and George the Giraffe were once again enjoying their afternoon in the sun, doing what they loved the most, sitting on their deckchairs and taking in as many ultraviolet rays as possible.

"This is the life, hey, Eric?" said George, swallowing a mouthful of lemonade.

"Yeah... it's not bad," replied Eric, less than enthusiastic.

"What's up?" asked George.

"Oh, it's nothing," replied Eric.

"Come on, tell me; you've been a bit down today. What's bothering you?" asked George.

"Well I've been wondering, Georgie-boy, don't you wish you could have done something with yourself?" said Eric.

"What do you mean?" replied George, puzzled.

"Well, look at us, we waste the days sitting on the lawn, never able to afford to do the things we've always dreamed of because we're always broke, and being looked upon by everyone as lazy," explained Eric.

"I never looked at it like that, Eric..." replied George. "Now that you've mentioned it, you're right!"

"Lately, I've been watching everyone going off to work, and it's made me wonder how nice it would be to have some sort of purpose in life," said Eric.

"What do you suggest we do? Find a job? We've already tried that and it didn't work!" replied George.

"I was thinking of doing something along the lines of a business of some sort," said Eric.

"How about selling your tropical fruit juices again? You made a bit of money last time," replied George.

"It was only to Leo and a few animals around the jungle; there was not exactly a mad rush to buy my juices," said Eric.

"What if you take your juices around the world? I'm sure you'd make loads of money then," said George.

"That sounds like a good idea, Georgie-boy!" replied Eric, feeling a bit more optimistic. "Maybe you could do the selling for me; you're good at talking..."

"What? Be your partner?" replied George.

"Yeah! If I invent the drinks, you could go and sell it all over the world!" said Eric. "How about it?"

"I'd love to!" answered George.

"Great! This time next year, Georgie-boy, we'll be millionaires," said Eric joyfully.

"I like the sound of that!" replied George excitedly.

George and Eric spent the rest of the day out on the lawn but the next day, and the next few days, there was no sign of them on the lawn. Instead, Eric was busy making lots of different kinds of juices, while George found customers after customers, landing big contract after contract. In fact, everyone all over the world knew about Eric and George's tropical fruit juice. No-one in the Karoomba jungle ever called them lazy again; in fact, what Eric and George learnt was that being lazy and inactive never amounted to anything. Eric's predictions came to pass and, after a year, they had made well over a million each. So, whenever you open your fridge... look closely, look very closely. You just might find one of Eric and George's tropical fruit juices inside...!

The End

The Bible teaches us to work hard and not to be lazy. When we work hard in school, or in our jobs, we will achieve better things and, whatever we do, we should do it with enthusiasm, as if we are working for God. We also need to respect and obey our teachers or our employers, and serve them like we serve God, whether they are watching or not. If you do this, it will please God, and He will reward you. We should also do the same when we work for God, whatever we do no; matter how big or small, it is never in vain, but worth something in His eyes.

Proverbs 13:4, Romans 12:11, Ephesians 6:5-8, 1 Corinthians 15:58.

GOODBYE

Well, that it is for now! I hope you enjoyed the tales and have learnt much from the misfortunes of the many animals in the Karoomba jungle. I can assure you that no animal was harmed in any of the tales, and that they continue causing mayhem and mischief... and you can guess who's at the centre of it all. Yep, you guessed it: Lenny. George and Eric, of course, are also right in the thick of it all...

And that, my friend, is another tale.